Piper reached for her purse. She had the business card in there somewhere. She felt something in the bottom of her purse that she didn't recognize.

Piper's eyebrows rose in surprise as she lifted out a red ribbon, knotted in the middle. Where did this come from? she wondered.

She was just reaching for the phone to call information when she heard a vibrating sound behind her. She turned to see a tall metal shelving unit, loaded with heavy canned goods, teetering.

She watched in shock as it began to fall toward her. Piper threw up her hands—a reaction that usually froze time.

But the shelving continued to fall. For the space of a heartbeat, Piper felt stuck in place, unable to summon the power that would save her.

She screamed as the shelf swayed forward and the heavy cans tumbled through the air.

What's happening to me? Piper asked herself. What's going on with my powers? Why didn't they work?

Titan Books a division of the Titan Publishing Group Ltd for premium use. For further information or classroom use write to: Special Markets Dept., Pocket Books, 1230 Avenue of the Americas, 5th Floor, New York, NY 10020-1586.

For information about special discounts for bulk purchases, please contact: Simon & Schuster Special Sales at 1-800-456-6798 or business@simonandschuster.com.

Charmed™

The Power of Three
A novelization by Eliza Willard

Kiss of Darkness
By Brandon Alexander

The Crimson Spell
By F. Goldsborough

Pocket Pulse
Published by Pocket Books

THE
CRIMSON SPELL

An original novel by F. Goldsborough
Based on the hit TV series
created by Constance M. Burge

A Parachute Press Book

POCKET PULSE

New York London Toronto Sydney Singapore

This book is a work of fiction. Names, characters, places and incidents are products of the author's imagination or are used fictitiously. Any resemblance to actual events or locales or persons, living or dead, is entirely coincidental.

An *Original* Publication of POCKET BOOKS

 POCKET PULSE published by
Pocket Books, a division of Simon & Schuster Inc.
1230 Avenue of the Americas, New York, NY 10020

™ & © 2000 Spelling Television Inc. All Rights Reserved.

ISBN: 0-671-04164-9

First Pocket Pulse printing April 2000

10 9 8 7 6 5 4 3 2 1

POCKET PULSE and colophon are trademarks of Simon & Schuster Inc.

Printed in the U.S.A.

THE
CRIMSON SPELL

PROLOGUE

The Master stood before a high table draped in dark velvet. Like all the others in the room, he wore a long, hooded black robe over his large frame and a deadly, double-edged dagger at his waist. Light from the dozens of black candles lining the room flickered, catching his green eyes. They glinted beneath his cowl like twin flames, seemingly without a face.

The house on Colwood Street had once been one of San Francisco's finest. It still had its high, vaulted ceilings and marble floors, but its tall windows were now boarded over, its elegant furniture was gone, and the marble floors were hidden beneath layers of filth. The house was abandoned, declared a hazard, slated for demolition—and yet, tonight it was filled with the black-robed

1

figures, their shadows dancing along the crumbling walls.

"Tonight is a time for both endings and beginnings," the Master's voice boomed through the parlor room. "There is someone who professed herself to be a member of our family. Only now have I discovered that she is a witch—one who opposes us!"

A collective gasp sounded in the room.

"Tonight her duplicity ends," the Master proclaimed. "And we initiate a new member into the coven. Let us begin."

He began a series of chants in Latin. The others joined in. As the chants continued, the master warlock cast herbs into a smoking urn on the table. To the herbs he added a vial of blood, the legs of a tarantula, and an orange powder that gave off a vile smell. The chanting continued, growing stronger.

Using the tip of his dagger, the Master drew a complex sign in the air above his head. As he finished, the dagger began to glow. Green lightning streaked out of the tip. It flew toward a crystal that hung in the center of the room.

The lightning enveloped the crystal, sizzling around it. The crystal became illuminated, shedding a hazy white light over the dark room.

"We are ready," the Master declared. "Bring in the witch."

Two of the coven members left and returned with a young woman who was bound and gagged. They dragged her to the front of the room and pushed her down so that she knelt before the Master. He signaled to the warlock beside her to remove the cloth gag.

"This is your last chance, witch," he said to her. "Do you serve the powers of Darkness? Will you swear your obedience to the coven?"

The young woman continued to strain against the ropes that bound her. "Never!" She spat at the ground at the Master's feet.

"You will regret that," the leader growled. "Place her beneath the crystal!"

"No!" the young woman cried. "Please!" The coven members at her side carried her. They shoved her down beneath the glowing crystal.

The Master began a new chant. Again the coven echoed his words. The chant intensified, becoming faster, louder. The crystal glowed intensely. A blinding light filled the room.

"Noooooo!" the witch screamed. Her body jerked in pain. She held up her hands to shield herself from the light.

The skin on her palms began to burn and bubble. The bubbles broke open, revealing muscle and bone underneath. She shrieked as her skin slid away, dripping down her arms like wax in a fire. The muscle and bone also began to liquefy, dripping onto her face, burning it, causing it, too, to dissolve.

A final screech of pain escaped the woman's lips. It turned into a sickening gurgle as her face melted completely. Her body collapsed—dripping—until all that was left of the woman was a pool of muck on the floor.

The white crystal radiated energy like a small sun.

"As we will it, so it must be," the Master said. "The crystal has captured the power of the witch. And now her power is ours." His flickering green eyes scanned the room. "Adrienne," he ordered, "bring in the new initiate."

A young woman with a long, ash-blond braid left the room. Moments later she returned with a handsome, powerfully built young man. He was stripped of his clothing to the waist.

"Kenji Yamada," the leader intoned. The young man knelt before the altar. "Are you ready to become a member—a warlock of the Coven of the New Sun?"

"I am," the young man answered.

The Master put his forefinger into the embers beneath the cauldron, then used the ashes to draw an inverted pentagram on the young man's bare chest.

"Hold out your hand," the leader ordered.

The initiate obeyed, and the Master nodded. Adrienne stepped to his side. She drew her dagger out of the sash at her waist and slashed it across the young man's palm.

Kenji cried out in surprise. He closed his fist tightly. Another warlock stepped up and placed a golden chalice beneath the fist, catching every drop of Kenji's spilling blood.

"You are now bound to us," the leader intoned. "By the dark of moon, water, earth and sky, wind and fire. Your blood is mingled with ours."

The young man didn't flinch, but repeated the words. "By the dark of moon, water, earth and sky, wind and fire."

"Do you swear to obey, to do our will without question or hesitation?" the Master asked.

"I swear to obey, to do the will of the coven without question or hesitation," Kenji responded.

"Do you understand and accept these terms: If you break your vow or betray the coven, the price will be your life?"

The young man hesitated for a fraction of a second before responding, "I accept that if I break my vow or betray the coven, the price will be my life."

"Rise," the leader commanded. A black robe was draped over the young man's shoulders. "You may take your place among the other members of the coven." The young man got to his feet and stepped back into the throng.

"Now," the leader went on, "there is another matter we must address tonight. Something very important—the greatest threat yet to our existence." He paused. "I have learned of three sisters. They are witches descended of a long and powerful lineage, who have only recently come into their gifts. Their combined powers are stronger than any that we have ever encountered. And they are committed to doing good—to protecting the innocent. If they find us before we find them, they will try to destroy us." He turned to face the crystal and raised his hands to it. "Therefore we have no choice. We must find them, destroy them first, and claim their powers for our own!"

A young man in the back of the room spoke up. "If they're so powerful, how do we fight them?"

The Master turned to face him. "We must get close to them, discover exactly what their powers are, then turn those powers against them. I will need you, my little spiders, to lure them into our web. Some of you have already made contact." His eyes landed on Kenji. "You will help us with this mission as part of your initiation, Kenji. Do you understand?"

"I understand," Kenji answered.

"Good." The Master smiled. "The work begins tonight."

CHAPTER 1

Piper Halliwell gazed around in dismay. I'll be here until dawn, she thought as she surveyed the mess. It was one A.M., and P3, her club, had just closed for the night. The tables were littered with hors d'oeuvre plates, the bar with beer bottles and glasses. Only the stage was clear, with no trace of the rocking Brazilian percussion band that had brought down the house earlier.

Hearing hot new bands was definitely the best part of Piper's new career move; cleaning up was not.

Whose brilliant idea was it that I should open this place? Oh, right. Piper giggled. Mine.

She took in a deep breath and reached for a tray. If she didn't get started, she'd never be able to get home and into bed. As she reached for a dirty plate, a loud knock at the door made her jump.

Who could that be? Piper wondered. She felt a little uneasy closing alone, and there wasn't much activity on the street at this hour on a Tuesday night. Wait, Piper corrected herself as she glanced at her watch and crossed to the glass front door, make that Wednesday morning.

She peered through the iron grillwork security gate and felt herself relax when she saw her sisters, Prue and Phoebe, standing in the fine, misty rain, grinning at her.

Piper opened the door, then unlocked the gate with a weary smile. "What are you two doing here?" she asked. "Shouldn't you be asleep?"

Phoebe pushed back the hood on her fleece jacket and stepped inside. "I wish," she complained. "For some reason, I couldn't sleep. So I went downstairs to see if anything was on TV and found Prue already there—"

"I couldn't sleep either," Prue explained. She finger-combed her dark, damp hair. She shrugged. "I've been kind of restless all day."

"So we thought we'd come visit you," Phoebe said. "You know, do a little sisterly catching up. And, uh, check up on our investment. Which, by the way, is looking a little shabby."

Piper smiled. It was because of her sisters that she was able to have P3. They helped her fund the place—and now that it was open, it was a huge success. Piper could never have done it without them. "You two are definitely nuts coming out here this late, but"—she gestured to the chaotic room around her—"welcome to my mess."

Prue's nose wrinkled with disdain. "Aren't the buspeople and waiters supposed to clean this up?"

"Yeah," Phoebe agreed. "Don't you get to skip the grunt work? I mean, you *are* the boss."

"Normally, yes. And my staff is great. But weeknights we have a skeleton crew, and Joey, the busboy, cut his hand open on a broken bottle at the end of the night, so Laura and Craig—the waitress and bartender—took him to the ER."

"Ooh." Prue grimaced. "That's awful."

"He'll be okay," Piper assured her. "As for me, the cook cleaned up the kitchen. All I really have to do is get the dishes into the dishwasher, the bottles into recycling, and then wipe down the tables and bar."

Prue took off her raincoat, revealing a gray shirt and black sweatpants underneath. "Well, I guess you've got your cleanup crew," she said with a sigh. She shot Phoebe a dark look. "I ought to know better by now. Every time I go along with one of your ideas, I wind up regretting it," she joked.

Phoebe gave Prue a look of wounded innocence and took off her fleece jacket. She was wearing a baby-blue flannel pajama top over loose navy sweatpants. "How was I supposed to know Piper was stuck with a mountain of dirty dishes?"

"Hello? Aren't you supposed to be able to 'see' things?" Prue asked.

"You know I can't control my visions," Phoebe

countered. "Unlike the two of you, who can use your powers whenever you want!"

"Speaking of which," Piper interrupted the conversation before it turned into a bickering contest. "Have either of you guys noticed how little we've needed to use our powers lately? It's been totally quiet. No warlocks or ghosts, no weird spirits—absolutely nothing out of the ordinary."

"I've been thinking the same thing," Prue said. "It's nice to get a break from all that, but I keep wondering when the next demon is going to pop up. All this peace and quiet . . . I don't trust it."

Piper shook her head. How twisted, she thought. For us, life is strange when it's *normal*. She thought back to how simple everything had been before Phoebe discovered *The Book of Shadows* in their attic. The book, a compilation of spells written down by their ancestors, was the first hint that the Halliwell sisters were witches. When Phoebe read one of those spells aloud—not so long ago, Piper realized—the girls' powers were activated.

The powers themselves were pretty cool. Phoebe had visions of the future—and occasionally the past. Prue's power was telekinesis, the ability to move objects with her mind. And Piper could freeze time, which was very handy in the right circumstances. But there was a definite downside, especially since their powers seemed to be a magnet for evil spirits.

Phoebe rolled her eyes. "Come on, guys. This

break is great. I finally have time to do some of the things I've always wanted to do."

Prue raised an eyebrow. "Like getting a job, I hope?" she asked.

Piper sighed. Prue didn't mean to be tough on Phoebe. She just didn't understand that her younger sister could be perfectly content hanging out, unemployed. So she hounded Phoebe about finding a job—daily—and usually started big arguments in the process.

Phoebe shot Prue a nasty look. "Actually, no. I'm taking karate classes. I started two weeks ago, and I am now officially a white belt."

"A white belt?" Piper repeated blankly. All she had ever heard of were black belts.

"That means I'm a beginner," Phoebe explained. "You start with a white belt and then progress through different colors until you reach black."

"Why didn't you tell us about this?" Prue asked.

"I was afraid I'd chicken out the first week," Phoebe admitted. "But now I'm totally into it. I'm learning basic punches, kicks, and blocks. Check this out." Phoebe gave a loud shout and punched the air to demonstrate.

"Looks like a real career move to me," Prue commented.

"Prue," Piper warned. "Don't start." She groaned as she lifted a heavy stack of dishes and carried them to the kitchen to place them in the dishwasher.

Phoebe stuck her chin in the air. "When we *do* run into a warlock or a demon, either of you guys can zap it with your powers and get away. But what about me? I'm defenseless!" she declared. "I'd say I'm doing something totally practical." She followed Piper, with another stack of dishes, into the kitchen.

"What about you?" Piper asked Prue when she returned to the club's main room. "Have *you* done anything interesting during this lull? I mean," she added with a smirk, "besides working, working, and working some more at Buckland's."

Buckland's was the downtown auction house where Prue worked—nearly nonstop, as far as Piper could tell—appraising antiques and putting together auctions.

"Well, I haven't signed up for any classes," Prue said. She tossed some dirty paper napkins into the trash. "But I have been doing some . . . research." She glanced at Piper. "Have you ever gone into Full Moon?"

Piper wiped down the glossy surface of the wooden bar. "The Wicca shop?"

"In Noe Valley?" Phoebe chimed in, returning from the kitchen.

Prue nodded. "I went in there a couple of weeks ago. I had a hot tip on an antique dagger that I wanted to include in my Medieval Treasures auction. Sure enough, the owner had the dagger—and it was authentic. After she sold it to me for a song, I started talking to her."

Piper narrowed her eyes, remembering the woman she had met the few times she'd been in the store. "The owner . . . is she the one with the long, blond braid? Wears a little silver pentagram? Looks kind of like Lady Guinevere?"

"That's the one," Prue said. "Her name's Adrienne. She knows a lot about herbs and traditional spells. And she stocks every bizarre ingredient you could imagine—henbane, monkshood, ague root, wood betony—"

"Eye of newt, toe of frog?" Phoebe teased.

Prue grinned. "Exactly. So we've been talking a lot about herbs and . . . things." She shrugged. "I don't know. She's just great. She's the first person I've met in ages I felt I could really open up to."

Phoebe's brown eyes went wide with alarm. "You didn't tell her about *us*—"

"Of course not!" Prue protested. "Adrienne thinks I practice Wicca, like most of the people who come into her shop."

"It's amazing how many people are into that," Phoebe commented as she began to clear another table.

"Wicca's not all that weird," Piper argued. "It celebrates the power of the earth and nature. And it's white magic. Part of a Wiccan's creed is to do no harm to anyone."

Prue sat down on the edge of the empty stage. "You know, before we got our powers, I always thought people who were into witchcraft were . . . I don't know . . ."

"Certifiable?" Phoebe guessed.

Prue smiled. "Something like that. And then once it became clear that *we* were witches, I just assumed we were the real thing and all the others were either con artists or acting out some fantasy role. But Adrienne is . . . different. She has really studied the history of magic. She's a walking textbook when it comes to using herbs. She seems really smart and down to earth."

Phoebe nudged Piper with her elbow. "Do you think it's possible that our sister—Miss I-Don't-Have-Time-for-Friendships—has actually found a friend?"

Piper laughed. "Let's not jump to any conclusions here."

"It's not easy to open up to someone when you're in our situation," Prue reminded them.

Piper hesitated, then decided. This was as good a moment as any to tell them something *she'd* been planning to participate in during her free time.

"I applied to be a mentor to a teen at risk." Piper let the words tumble out of her mouth. She pulled an envelope from her back pocket and fingered it nervously. "Today I got a letter from the Sunrise Center. I've been accepted and assigned to a kid."

"A kid?" Prue echoed, sounding alarmed.

"What's the Sunrise Center?" Phoebe asked.

Piper took the safe route and chose to answer Phoebe's question first. "It's a halfway house for teens who've been bounced from foster homes or juvenile facilities," she explained.

Prue frowned. "Juvenile facilities? As in, prisons?"

"Most of the kids at the Sunrise Center are there because they got a rough deal," Piper responded. "The Sunrise Center is where they're trying to pull it together, finish their high school courses or get jobs."

Phoebe and Prue exchanged a look that Piper couldn't decipher. "Ookay," Phoebe said, sounding cautious, "so what does a mentor do?"

"I'm assigned to be a kind of big sister to one of the kids there," Piper said. "I meet with her for a few hours every week and help with her homework or take her to a museum or go blading in the park—whatever she needs."

"Piper," Prue said. "I don't think this is a good idea. It means getting very close to a very needy kid. I hate to always be the heavy here, but do you really think it's wise to invite a stranger that far into our lives? One as unpredictable as a troubled teen? Besides, you'd be working under some serious restrictions. You couldn't even invite her over to the house."

"I realize all that." Piper kept her tone calm. She knew Prue would object without hearing her through, and she was prepared for it. "I realize we can't risk anyone finding *The Book of Shadows* or seeing us use our powers. But I don't have to bring her home. There are lots of places in the city for us to meet." She stopped talking as she realized that neither of her sisters looked convinced. "What it comes down to," she said firmly, "is that this is something *I'm* doing. It doesn't involve the three of us."

"I don't know about that." Phoebe took a seat on the stage, next to Prue. "I kind of agree with Prue here. What affects one of us, affects us all."

What? Piper stared at Phoebe. She couldn't believe her ears. She was sure her younger sister would back her up. Being a mentor at the Sunrise Center was a totally good cause.

"Look, all I'm talking about is one afternoon or evening a week that could make a very big difference to a kid who's never had much. I want to do it, and I'm going to." She crossed to a table and began clearing it, signaling to her sisters that the conversation was over.

Phoebe let out a yawn. "Two A.M. and we're still not done cleaning up," she groaned.

"And I've got to be at work tomorrow morning at eight," Prue said. She got to her feet and looked around. "Piper, do me a favor and open the big recycling bin in the back, okay?"

Piper's mouth dropped open. "What . . . you're not . . ."

Prue shrugged. A mischievous expression crossed her face. "I know we're not supposed to use our power for our own gain—but I'm actually helping *you*. So it's only cheating a little."

Suppressing a giggle, Piper dashed into the kitchen and opened the lid on the big blue recycling bin. She returned to the main room to see Prue focusing her ice-blue eyes on the tables before her—the ones littered with empty beer bottles. The bottles levitated, quivering in the air for a moment, then shot straight into the kitchen and dropped into the recycling bin.

Phoebe blinked in astonishment. "Whoa. Two points. Precision telekinesis. You ever think of going out for the Lakers? You'd be a natural, you know."

Prue just smiled. "Come on," she told her sisters. "Let's get out of here."

Piper stepped toward the kitchen to start the dishwasher, and a movement caught her eye. A shadowy figure stood at the window. "Who's there?" she cried. Prickles of fear tingled along the back of her neck.

"Where?" Phoebe asked.

Piper pointed toward the front window. "There. I saw someone standing there. Someone was watching us."

CHAPTER

2

Phoebe and Piper darted toward the window. "I don't see anyone," Phoebe reported.

"No. Look at the bushes," Piper said in a hushed tone. "The branches are all broken in one spot. As if someone pushed through them and was standing right there."

Prue joined her sisters at the window. Her face mirrored their worried expressions.

"Well, whoever was there is long gone by now." Prue sighed. "Let's just go home and get some sleep."

"It was pretty dark in here," Phoebe suggested in a bright tone. "And we're not even sure if Piper saw a person, a dog . . ."

Or a warlock, Piper added silently. She grabbed her keys and ushered her sisters out of the club. "I'm not sure, guys, but I hope our nice, quiet period hasn't just ended."

Later that morning Phoebe sat beside Piper in the car, giving her sister directions. "It's around the corner, second building on the left," Phoebe instructed.

Earlier Phoebe's car had totally refused to start. And since she'd been running late, Piper had offered to drop her off at her class. "There! That little storefront with the Japanese lettering in the window—that's my dojo."

Phoebe felt a surge of energy just looking at the place. I'm so glad I decided to do this for myself, she thought. It's so empowering. So positive.

Piper pulled to a stop in front of the karate school and yawned. "I'm still recovering from last night's cleanup. How do you have the energy for a karate class when none of us got more than five hours of sleep?"

Phoebe reached into the backseat for her gym bag. "Prue went off to Buckland's this morning," she reminded her sister. "She got less sleep than I did."

"That's because Prue is an automaton," Piper grumbled. She flashed Phoebe a grin. "But don't tell her I said so."

"Your secret's safe with me," Phoebe promised. She got out of the car and leaned in the window. "Thanks for the ride."

Piper nodded toward a tall, burly man walking into the dojo. "Somehow I just can't imagine you kicking that guy's butt."

Phoebe grinned. "Neither can I, but I'm working on it."

She waved as her sister drove away, then jogged toward the dojo. She bowed as she entered, and signed in for her class at the front desk.

Two of the more senior students, dressed in white karate uniforms tied with brown belts, sparred with each other in the middle of the floor. Watching them, Phoebe fought down a case of nerves. This was her first all-levels class after two weeks of white-belts-only, beginner's classes. She hoped she'd be able to keep up with the more advanced students.

Who am I kidding? Phoebe thought. I'm just hoping I don't make a total fool of myself.

In the women's locker room, Phoebe changed into her karate uniform, or *gi*, heavy white cotton drawstring pants and a kimono-style jacket. Then she took out the stiff white cloth belt and knotted it around her waist. Next to her, an elderly woman—probably around seventy years old—knotted a green belt around her waist. Phoebe smiled to herself. Even "grandma" here can wipe the floor with me, she realized. But someday—someday soon—I'll be a color belt, too.

She stepped out onto the dojo floor and bowed again. She took a spot well away from the sparring brown belts and began stretching. Each exercise made her feel stronger and more relaxed.

Phoebe was bent over one leg, working on her calf muscles, when she noticed a shadow on the floor. Someone was standing beside her. She glanced up—and felt her jaw drop open. Whoa! Serious hottie alert! A young man, probably in his early twenties, stood reaching up to the ceiling. His gleaming, black shoulder-length hair was tied back, highlighting his high cheekbones and tanned skin. His dark eyes seemed intense—focused on his exercise. Even though he wore a loose-fitting gi she could see that he had a lean, muscular build. He wore a white belt.

A white belt! Phoebe thought, which means *he's in my class!*

He glanced at Phoebe, smiled, and gave her a slight bow. Phoebe stood up and bowed back. She bit her lip, fighting a goofy smile. Weird. This may be the first time I've ever flirted with a guy by *bowing* to him!

Sensei Towers, a young Jamaican man with a third-degree black belt, walked onto the floor. Well, so much for starting a conversation, Phoebe realized. She lined up with the rest of the students, everyone bowed to the instructor, and the class began.

Phoebe was relieved that the first thing Sensei had them do was kneel and meditate. *That* she could handle. The stretching and warm-up exercises were fine, too, though she found herself distracted, sneaking peeks at the new student.

He moved like a gymnast, she decided. She watched him go into an optional full-split exercise.

And limber, too. He'd advance through the belts very quickly. She didn't need to have a vision to see that!

Next everyone lined up by rank, and Sensei gave each color-belt group a series of exercises to do. The white belts were assigned a drill of three punches and three blocks. All the beginners performed the moves in sync.

Punch, block, punch, block, punch, block. So far so good, Phoebe thought. I've managed to keep the humiliation factor to a minimum. And— bonus—I don't look like an uncoordinated klutz in front of superguy over here.

"Yamada, put some force behind that punch!" Sensei barked. "Focus!"

Phoebe glanced over at the new guy and stopped her routine in surprise. He was moving with the power and precision of an advanced student. He even nailed that little twist of the wrist on each punch, which none of the other white belts had mastered.

"Phoebe, why aren't you blocking?" Sensei Towers demanded.

"Oh, I am," Phoebe replied quickly. She threw up her right arm.

"*Left* block!" the teacher corrected loudly. "Left block!" Phoebe felt her face flush as she switched arms and scrambled to keep up with the rest of the class.

"Left high block, right middle punch, left low block," she murmured, trying to keep the sequence straight. Her eyes found the new student again. He was doing the sequence perfectly.

"Phoebe." Sensei Towers now stood directly in front of her. "What seems to be the problem?"

I'm too busy drooling over superguy to concentrate, Phoebe thought. "The low block," she said, covering. "I keep thinking my left arm should go down."

"It does."

"But first your left hand has to sweep *up* toward your right ear," Phoebe explained. "I get confused."

A hint of a smile played at Sensei's mouth. "Kenji, come here please," he said.

The new guy came to stand beside her. Kenji, Phoebe thought. She felt a little shiver in her spine. So that's your name: Kenji Yamada.

Sensei Towers nodded at him. "Please enlighten Ms. Halliwell."

"Certainly. Follow me," Kenji said.

To the ends of the earth, Phoebe thought. She smiled for a second at her own silliness, then focused on the drill. Kenji moved slowly so that Phoebe could follow the sequence from start to finish. This time she got it. "Good," he complimented her, his grin wide.

Even his voice is attractive, Phoebe realized. Deep and soft.

"Let's work on a little self-defense," Sensei Towers called out. "Pair up for combination number one." He glanced at Phoebe and Kenji. "You two continue working together."

Self-defense combinations, Phoebe had learned, were a series of moves designed to get you out of specific street situations. Most martial arts schools didn't include them in their lessons, but it was exactly the kind of instruction Phoebe was looking for. She was glad Sensei Towers saw the value of them, too.

In combination number one, she reminded herself, an "attacker" grabs you from behind, and you try to break out of their arms.

"Ready?" Kenji asked.

"Ready." Phoebe had to stop herself from grinning like a fool. How perfect! If she had to pick one person she'd like to grab her, Kenji was definitely the guy.

Kenji stepped behind Phoebe and put his arms around her. She could smell the sharp citrus scent of his aftershave. She let herself lean back against him and could almost feel an electrical current running between them.

"Go!" Sensei Towers called.

Wham! Phoebe hit the floor. Her head spun. What just happened?

Kenji gazed down at her, concern in his dark eyes. "Are you all right?" he asked.

Phoebe nodded and got to her feet. She rubbed her hip. Ow! Sometimes love hurts, she thought ruefully.

"You were supposed to break out of my arms and take me down," Kenji explained. "Let's try it again."

With pleasure! Phoebe thought as he wrapped his arms around her.

"Now, what you're supposed to do is stamp

down on my instep with your heel, use your hands in a scissors move to push my arms apart, step out, pivot, sweep my ankle, and—" Kenji led her through the movements in slow motion. Phoebe watched, feeling nearly entranced by the fluid movement of his body. He fell expertly to the ground. "Now you finish me off with a jab to the throat."

"I think I'll let you off easy this time," Phoebe joked. She held out her hand to help him to his feet. "I don't understand. What's your secret? How did you get so good for a beginner?"

"Tell you after class," Kenji promised. He winked at her.

Phoebe's heart thumped. After class? That sounded interesting!

The rest of the lesson was reserved for *kata*— the choreographed fights against imaginary opponents. After several drills, Phoebe sat down to watch the other color belts. When the brown belts were called up, Sensei nodded to Kenji.

Phoebe's eyes widened as he joined them and flawlessly executed the complicated series of kicks, jumps, and strikes. Move over, Jackie Chan! she thought. Who *is* this guy?

When class ended, Phoebe hurried through the required cleanup of the dojo, then dressed quickly. She checked her reflection in the dressing room mirror. She was wearing an olive-green knit camisole, a matching sweater, and black bootleg pants. Not her sexiest outfit, but it would do. After all, she reminded herself, the guy had already seen her in her unflattering gi. This ensemble was definitely an improvement.

She bowed as she left the dojo, then stepped outside. Just as she hoped, Kenji stood waiting for her on the sidewalk. He had changed into a black T-shirt and black jeans—tight enough to reveal just how buff he was.

"Want to get a cup of coffee?" he asked.

"Make it an iced tea, and you're on," Phoebe said. "I know this great new café called Leaf and Bean. It's just down the street, and they have the yummiest teas ever."

"Sounds great." Kenji smiled—the most stunning smile Phoebe had ever seen.

They began walking toward the shop. The fog was in from the bay again, and the air had turned cool. Phoebe pulled her cardigan more tightly around her. "So, hi. I'm Phoebe—"

"I know who you are, Phoebe Halliwell," Kenji told her.

Phoebe frowned. "Wait—how do you—"

"Sensei must have said your name five times during class," he explained.

"Okay then, mystery boy, since you know who I am, it's time for you to spill," she demanded. "Who are you? Where do you come from? And what kind of white belt knows all the brown belt moves and can demonstrate them almost as well as the teacher?"

Kenji grinned. "My name is Kenji Yamada. I'm from San Diego. I just moved here last week." He leaned in closer. "And here's my biggest secret—I have a brown belt in another style. I trained in San Diego for five years. This style is very similar to the one I studied, but Sensei Towers wanted me to start from the ground up."

"Bummer," Phoebe empathized.

"Oh, it's okay. It's pretty common to do that when you switch schools," Kenji explained.

"Here we are," Phoebe announced. "The Leaf and Bean Café." They entered the little storefront and quickly snagged a table by the window. The two of them glanced over the menu of herbal teas. Each herb had a description of the spiritual or healing properties it was supposed to possess.

Kind of like the ingredients in *The Book of Shadows*, Phoebe realized. Maybe that's why she liked this place so much.

A waitress came over and asked for their order. "I'll have the Chai iced tea," Phoebe decided.

"Will any of these teas make me invincible?" Kenji asked.

The waitress shot him a strange look. "Excuse me?"

"Never mind. I'll take a green tea, hot, straight up."

"Invincible?" Phoebe asked when the waitress had gone.

"Yeah. Today Sensei told me that he's put me in an intermediate fight class and"—he winced—"entered me in a tournament."

"A tournament? Wow!" Phoebe couldn't imagine ever being good enough to actually compete against other people.

"There's a big meet in Oakland this weekend for all the schools in the Bay Area. Sensei says that if I'm serious about going for a black belt, I've got to start competing again."

"So you've done this before?"

"Sure, until last year," Kenji explained. "Then I got obsessed with getting into grad school and stopped training as hard. So my fighting's pretty rusty."

Phoebe put her hand on Kenji's arm to reassure him. He didn't seem out of practice to her.

Bright light flashed into her eyes. She felt the jolt of energy that always signaled a premonition. Yes. It was happening. Images flowed into her mind:

Kenji in the fight ring, moving lightly and easily.

Kenji attacking his opponent with a lightning-fast technique.

The opponent striking. Kenji's head snapping back—taking a nasty kick to the jaw.

The scene shifted. Cheering. A grinning Kenji holding up a second-place trophy.

Phoebe blinked as the images faded. The vision was over. She smiled.

"Earth to Phoebe?" Kenji said.

"Huh?" Uh-oh. How spaced out was I during that premonition? she wondered. Better cover fast. "Umm—just looking for the waitress. Can't wait to get that tea."

"Yeah. I'm hoping that the"—he glanced at the

menu—"*centering properties* of the green tea will help me focus for the tournament."

The waitress returned and set two glasses on the table. Phoebe twirled her iced tea with a straw. "This one's supposed to give you balance and tranquility."

"I should probably stock up on that," he joked. "To drink after I make a fool of myself in the tournament."

Phoebe smiled as she remembered Kenji's proud expression in her vision. "You don't have anything to worry about," Phoebe declared.

"Oh, really." Kenji raised an eyebrow. "So you recommend a calm approach to getting your teeth kicked in?"

Phoebe bit her lip. Kenji seemed so nervous. Should she give him a hint about her vision? Let him know what she saw?

Why not? she decided. What's it going to hurt?

She leaned close to him. "Trust me. It's going to be okay. In fact, I think you can count on getting at least second place."

Kenji's dark eyes narrowed at her. "What makes you so sure of that?"

Phoebe straightened, suddenly uncomfortable with the secret she shared. Big mouth strikes again, she scolded herself. Time for damage control.

She laughed loudly, as if Kenji had said something funny. "Oh, I'm not *sure*, silly." She slapped him lightly on the arm. "I mean, it's not like I can read the future or anything."

"You've never seen me compete," Kenji countered. His gaze grew more intense. "How can you say I'll win second place?"

"Sensei would never have entered you in the tournament if he didn't think you could win," Phoebe protested. There, she thought. Finally a logical argument.

"I guess you have a point," Kenji conceded. "So will you be at the tournament cheering me on?"

Phoebe's heart fluttered a little. He was inviting her to come and see him!

Oh, no! She had plans for Saturday—to help Prue clean out the basement. Ugh! "I'm sorry. I've got another commitment," she confessed.

"I see." Kenji took a sip of tea.

Phoebe couldn't tell if he was disappointed. "Besides," she teased, "you'll probably be so caught up in the tournament that you wouldn't even notice if I was there."

Kenji lifted his smoldering eyes to Phoebe's and held her gaze. "Believe me. I'd notice," he assured her.

Phoebe felt her face begin to grow warm. "Sooo," she said, trying to recover from her blush. "Why did you leave San Diego?"

"Berkeley. It's got one of the greatest graduate programs in engineering in the country," he explained. "Are you in school?"

"No. I just moved back to San Francisco. I was living in New York, but I came back because my sisters and I inherited my grandmother's house."

Kenji's eyebrows rose. "A whole house? Sounds nice."

"We all grew up there, so we love the place. It's one of those big, old, funky Victorians."

"I'm in a tiny student apartment in Berkeley," Kenji confessed. "Not big on atmosphere, but it's close to campus and affordable." He shrugged. "I'll probably spend most of the year staring at a computer screen anyway." He gave Phoebe another long, lingering gaze. "Then again, maybe I won't spend *all* my time at my desk," he confided.

This time Phoebe didn't look away. Her gaze met his as she basked in his attention. "Really?" she said in a flirtatious tone. "Why's that?"

A slow smile spread across Kenji's face. "Let's just say there's a lot more I want to get to know about Phoebe Halliwell."

CHAPTER
3

Piper stood in front of the Sunrise Center, a large
wood-shingled house a few miles from Halliwell
Manor. She had been standing there for a full five
minutes.

She hoped that what she was about to do was
a good thing, both for the girl she'd been
assigned to and for herself. She had felt very certain about being a mentor while she was arguing
with Prue and Phoebe. Now that she was really
about to do it, a nagging doubt crept through her.

Come on, get a grip, Piper coached herself. She
flicked her dark hair back over her shoulders,
took a breath, and pressed the buzzer with as
much confidence as she could muster.

A tall, fatherly-looking man with thick salt-and-
pepper hair and wire-rimmed glasses answered
the door. "Can I help you?"

"I'm Piper Halliwell—"

"Of course! You signed up for our mentor program." He held out a hand to her, giving her a warm smile. "I'm Justin Morgan, coordinator for the Sunrise Center. Please come in."

Here goes, Piper thought. She followed Mr. Morgan into the large building. Sunlight streamed in through ceiling skylights and down onto the linoleum floors. Mr. Morgan led Piper past what looked like a living room and a large room with picnic tables and benches that was obviously the dining hall.

Although the halfway house seemed clean and well cared for, Piper's nose wrinkled at the institutional odor of the place—too much disinfectant and steam-table food. It hardly smelled like a home. A feeling of gratitude welled up inside Piper. She and her sisters were lucky never to have wound up in a place like this. And they were doubly lucky to have had Grams—and one another.

"You can have a full tour later if you'd like," Mr. Morgan said. "But first I'd like to talk to you about the program."

He led Piper into his office—a tidy room furnished with a large desk, a tall metal filing cabinet, and several comfortable-looking chairs.

"Have a seat," he said. "Did you read the literature we sent you?"

"Every bit of it. At least twice," Piper told him. She bit her lip, then decided it was best to be honest about her concerns. "Mr. Morgan, I think the mentoring program is really great, but I have to tell you I've had a few doubts about whether or not this is the right thing for me to do. I have a pretty demanding job—and a some-times demanding family—and I honestly don't know how much I can be around for one of these kids."

Mr. Morgan gazed directly at her. "Can you manage two hours a week?"

"Two hours—that's all?" she asked.

Mr. Morgan smiled warmly, his eyes twink-ling. "I have to warn you, though. These kids are pretty compelling. Many of the mentors become very involved with them and wind up giving up much more of their time than they expected. But we *require* that you give only two hours."

"That sounds manageable," Piper admitted.

"We want the kids to have a connection in the outside world," Mr. Morgan explained. "Some-one with a life beyond the halfway house. Partly so they can have a role model."

For a moment Piper wondered what Mr. Morgan would think of having a witch as a role model for one of his charges. Maybe Prue was right. Maybe this wasn't such a good idea.

"Someone who holds a job in the community," Mr. Morgan continued. "Whose life doesn't re-volve around buying or selling drugs, someone very different from what these kids are used to. But really, the most important thing is that these girls feel they matter to someone. Without a car-ing family around, it's easy for these kids to get lost."

Mr. Morgan's words hit home. *This* was why Piper wanted to volunteer in the first place: to share the good in her life with someone who was less fortunate. Witch or not, she was certainly capable of that. Piper nodded. "I can do it. Or at least," she added, "I can try."

"Good." The director smiled at her. "Are you ready to meet the girl we've assigned to you? Her name is Celeste. She's been with us for about three months." He handed Piper a bio on the girl. She skimmed it quickly.

"What if I can't get her to trust me?" she asked. "What if we never really connect? What if I'm a terrible mentor?"

"That's negative thinking," Mr. Morgan chided her. "Remember, these kids *want* a connection. They're aching for it. So, think positively and allow it to happen. It will."

Piper nodded.

"Now, enough with the suspense," Mr. Morgan said. "Let me introduce you to Celeste."

He led her to a small room off the main hall. A girl sat in a swivel chair, her feet on the windowsill, staring out the window. "Hello, Celeste," he said.

At the sound of his voice, the girl spun the chair around. A flicker of interest flashed in her pale blue eyes when she saw Piper. It was almost immediately replaced by something else. Wariness? Piper guessed. Nervousness?

Celeste was slight and looked closer to ten than to thirteen, the age listed on her bio. She wore her fine, reddish blond hair cropped short. Her striped long-sleeved T-shirt was several sizes too big for her, as were her faded overalls.

And, Piper noticed, she still hadn't said a word.

"Hi." Piper started to hold out her hand to shake, then changed her mind. Too uncool. "I'm Piper Halliwell."

"Celeste Bailey," the girl replied.

Mr. Morgan smiled. "Well, I'll leave you two to get acquainted."

He's leaving? So soon? Piper tried not to look completely panicked. She'd been hoping he'd stay at least for a few moments. Though Piper didn't detect any outright hostility, Celeste definitely had a cool and challenging air about her.

The door to the room clicked closed behind Mr. Morgan. Piper sank into the folding chair across from Celeste. "So . . ." she began awkwardly. She stopped when she realized her brain was a total blank. What should she say now?

Celeste just stared at her, not helping at all.

Okay, think, Piper ordered herself. She remembered a section in one of the center's pamphlets called, "What to talk about at your first mentoring meeting." It suggested things like, "Discuss who you are and what brought you to Sunrise."

"So, uh, I've been interested in joining a mentoring program for a while now," Piper offered.

"Yeah?" Celeste's interest level registered about a two on a scale of one to ten.

It would help if you asked me why, Piper thought, frustration rising in her. Then she realized—it was her job to make Celeste comfortable, not the other way around. You're the adult, she told herself. Act like one.

She forged on. "The thing is, I've always felt really lucky because I have two sisters. Our parents weren't around for very long. My dad took off after my youngest sister was born, and my mom died when we were all kind of young. But my sisters and I, we've always taken care of each other. I thought I'd like to help someone else in the same position we were in. Sort of return the favor."

Celeste nodded. Which was kind of a response, Piper thought. But only barely. Now what?

Piper glanced at the bio sheet she held. "This says you don't have parents either."

"I never knew them at all," Celeste said. "They died in a car accident a month after I was born. I'm what's known as a ward of the state." A bitter half-smile played across her lips.

"So you've been in other state institutions?" Not the happiest of topics, but it's a start, Piper figured.

"No, a lot of foster homes," Celeste explained. "The last one . . . the father had some

sick ideas about me. The social worker promised me a new placement. But I wasn't about to
wait. I cut out."

"And that's how you wound up here,"
Piper filled in. How sad—she could only imagine the kind of life Celeste had already had at
such a young age. No wonder she was hard to
reach.

Celeste's smile flickered again. "Well, yeah.
But first I got busted."

Piper wanted to ask what she'd been busted
for but decided she wasn't ready to go there yet.
Besides, she could always find out from Mr.
Morgan if she felt it was really important. And it
was a little fact that her sisters didn't need to
know about anyway.

"The judge gave me a choice," Celeste contin-
ued. "A correctional institution or the Sunrise
Center." She swiveled in the chair, palms raised.
"What would you choose?"

"Do you like it here?" Piper asked.

Celeste wrinkled her delicate nose. "It smells
funny and the food is total barf, but I guess it's all
right."

Celeste gazed down at her watch strap. She
began unbuckling and rebuckling it. That must
mean it's my turn again, Piper guessed.

"So—what do you like to do?" she asked, hoping to find some common ground. "You know,
for fun?"

"Fun?" Celeste echoed. She shrugged. "I don't
know . . . I read a lot. And I—" She stared down

at her hands. She gazed back up at Piper through her pale eyelashes. "I like to cook."

"To cook?" Yes! Piper wanted to shout. Could anything be more perfect? "I'm a cook! I mean, I was a chef at a restaurant. And then I bought this nightclub. We have a cool tapas menu there. And sometimes I still do private catering. I *love* to cook. It's practically my life." The words came out in a jumble.

"Really?" Celeste asked.

"Maybe we could cook together sometime," Piper suggested. "I could take you to my club during the day to use the kitchen there," she offered. "We've got a real brick oven and amazing equipment."

The girl just nodded. Uh-oh. Maybe I was too pushy. She decided to back off a little. "So are you in high school?" Piper asked, figuring that would be neutral territory.

Celeste shook her head. "I'm taking a couple of equivalency courses at the center."

"So you're thinking of going to college?"

The girl gave a bitter laugh. "No, I'm thinking of getting a job before I wind up standing in line at a soup kitchen."

Ugh. Strike two. Piper thought. I really stepped in it that time. "Look," she said, "I'm sorry if I'm asking a zillion questions. I'm not trying to interrogate you. I just want to get to know you a little so that maybe we can become friends." A thought occurred to her. "Have you been able to make any friends here at the center?"

"One," Celeste answered. "At least, I think I have one."

"What do you mean?"

Celeste's pale blue eyes met Piper's. "Mr. Morgan said they didn't get enough mentors to sign up, so my friend Daria got left without one. The dumb thing is, she's the one who really wanted a mentor—and she was pretty upset when I came down here to meet you."

"Oh." No wonder Celeste was having a hard time warming up to her, Piper realized. She was starting out with a major guilt trip. Then it hit her: the perfect solution! "Celeste, how would you feel if I mentored you *and* Daria—together?"

Celeste's blue eyes widened. "You would do that?"

"We'd have to clear it with Mr. Morgan first, but why not?" Piper shrugged. "The more the merrier."

For the first time Celeste really smiled, and Piper knew she'd said the right thing. It gave her a great feeling inside.

"That would be *so* cool," Celeste told her. She stood up. "Want to see my room?" she asked. "I share it with Daria. You can meet her. She will be totally psyched!"

"Sure!" Piper followed the girl up a stairway to the third floor. Then Celeste led her into a small, cramped room at the end of the hallway. Bunk beds were placed on one wall and a dresser painted bright orange stood across from it. A battered wooden desk and chair took up the third wall. Posters of different alternative bands were taped all over the place.

A young girl, whose chin-length dark hair was tinted blue, sat on the lower bunk, her back slumped against the wall. She wore a shapeless gray sweater over black cargo pants. If anyone could be the picture of bummed out, Piper observed, this girl was it.

"Hey," Celeste flopped down on the bed next to her roommate. "I want you to meet Piper, my mentor."

Daria lifted her head and glanced at Piper. "Hi," she said in a flat tone.

Celeste grinned at Piper, then at Daria. "By the way, she's *your* mentor, too," she announced.

Daria's eyes narrowed. "What are you talking about?"

"I told Piper about you, and she said she'd mentor us together!"

"You're messing with me, right?" Daria asked warily.

Piper walked toward her. "As long as it's okay with Mr. Morgan, the offer's for real," she said. "Are you interested?"

Daria's face lit up. "Yes!" she shouted. "Yes, yes, yes!" She sprang off the bed to give Piper a hug, nearly knocking her over. "I can't believe it! This is so totally, amazingly fantastic!"

Daria flung herself at Celeste and danced her around. Giggling, Daria hugged Piper again, then plopped onto the top of the desk. "Okay, mentor," she said, swinging her legs. "What do we do now? When do we meet and what are we gonna do and where are we gonna go?"

"Whoa, let's take those one at a time." Piper held up a hand. "How about if the three of us get together later this week—maybe the day after tomorrow? Daria, I told Celeste we could do a cooking session at my nightclub. We can make pizza—with the toppings of your choice. You okay with that?"

"You own a club? How cool is that? And pizza is like my all-time most favorite food in the entire world," Daria told her. "I am *so* okay with that!"

"What about you, Celeste?"

"Sounds great!" Celeste said.

Daria launched herself off the desk and opened the room's narrow closet. "Come on, Celeste. You have to help me pick out what I'm going to wear!"

Piper bit back a smile. Then, as Daria tore through the closet, Piper studied Celeste. She was so much quieter than her rocket-fueled roommate. It was hard to tell what she was really thinking. Piper had a feeling it would take a while before Celeste really let her in. Still, she seemed much happier now that Daria was part of the program, and Piper was glad she'd offered to mentor both of them.

There's only one problem, she thought ruefully. How am I ever going to explain this to my sisters? Prue and Phoebe hadn't wanted her to mentor even one girl—and now she had two!

Daria emerged from the closet. "I know," she declared. "I'll model a few outfits for you, and we can all decide what looks best. Then to celebrate, we'll all go out for ice cream, okay?"

Piper blinked. Did I say I was mentoring two girls? Make that two and a half!

CHAPTER
4

Maybe I was too hard on Piper about the mentoring thing, Prue thought. She strolled down Church Street to Twenty-fourth Street, enjoying the warm breeze on her face. It had been a long hike from Buckland's, which was in the center of the city, but the sky was a clear, brilliant blue and the temperature was perfect. This weather definitely warranted a walk.

She turned onto Twenty-fourth Street, Noe Valley's main drag. Twenty-fourth was a cheerful, busy street, lined with coffee houses, restaurants, bookstores, boutiques, and cute specialty shops. Plenty of window-shopping here, Prue thought, eyeing a display of whimsical kitchen utensils.

Maybe my sisters are right. Maybe I am being too guarded—and paranoid, Prue mused. What if I followed Piper's lead and started to be a little freer myself—let the walls down a little? She turned down a tiny alley that ran between two stores on Twenty-fourth. It was the only way to get to Full Moon. Prue considered the shop one of the city's better-kept secrets. There was no sign for it; you simply had to know it was there.

Appropriately mysterious for a store catering to those practicing magic, she thought. And its hidden quality was definitely part of its charm.

Prue remembered the first time she walked down this alley toward Full Moon. Then she'd had no interest in the Wicca store and all its trappings. She'd been on a mission to find the perfect final piece for her auction. Adrienne had given her that—and something more—a feeling of friendship that Prue hadn't experienced in a long time.

Later she'd discovered that Adrienne's store was well known among Wiccans. If you practiced white magic in the Bay Area, Full Moon was home ground.

The alley ended in a small, square, cobbled courtyard shaded by a California pepper tree. A redwood bench sat beneath the tree. A fountain made of slate and copper trickled beside it, and wind chimes rang softly in the breeze. Somehow, Prue thought, Adrienne had managed to turn a few square feet of city space into a miniature oasis. This was clearly a woman with positive energy.

Prue walked down the three steps that led into

the shop and opened the door. Adrienne glanced up from behind a redwood counter where she was talking on the phone. Her worried expression melted into a smile when she recognized Prue. She covered the phone with one hand. "Blessed be. I'll be with you in a minute."

"No hurry," Prue said. "I'll just look around."

Yeah, letting down the walls a little might feel really good, Prue realized. Especially with someone as smart and nice as Adrienne.

Prue wandered through the store's aisles, which were crammed with fascinating items. There were rune stones and Tarot cards, books on magic and witchcraft, candles, incense, crystals, shells, scented oils, chalices and cauldrons, the ritual daggers known as *athames*, and shelf after shelf of carefully labeled glass jars containing herbs, roots, seeds, powders—almost anything that might be called for in a spell.

Adrienne pushed her long, ash-blond braid off of her shoulder. It swung gracefully down her back. "No, I'm sorry, I don't stock them," she said firmly into the phone. "No, I don't know who would. Blessed be." She hung up.

"There's something you *don't* stock?" Prue asked in mock astonishment.

Adrienne gave the phone a disgusted look. "He wanted steel nails, black candles, and a cloth doll—the kind of stuff you use in a black magic spell to cause harm to someone. I wasn't about to aid and abet him in his task."

Prue tried not to seem too interested. "Do you

get a lot of those calls?" she asked. "You know, from people practicing black magic?"

Adrienne tucked a loose strand of hair behind her ear. "Not a lot. Most people who are into the Craft know that this shop is white magic only. Why?"

Prue shrugged, hoping she sounded casual. "Just curious, I guess."

Prue and her sisters had certainly had up close and personal experience with some seriously sinister warlocks. Sometimes she wondered just how many of them were out there, lurking, waiting for their opportunity to strike against the Charmed Ones. It was part of the reason for her paranoia. Prue's unofficial motto, "Trust no one," had come in handy on more than one occasion.

Adrienne leaned back against the counter and folded her arms. "Wherever there's light, there's also dark. The Chinese got it right centuries ago." She pointed to a yin-yang necklace in the display case. The ancient symbol showed dark and light as two halves of a circle, each fitting into and containing the seed of the other.

Maybe the symbol could teach Prue a lesson. There was just as much goodness and light in the world as evil. Goodness even she could enjoy. Prue frowned. Maybe her motto should change to "Trust someone—just be cautious about whom."

"So—what can I do for you?" Adrienne asked.

Prue was tempted to tell the truth, to say that she liked Adrienne, and that she had just dropped by to visit. But that felt . . . weird. Risky. It violated too many of her caution reflexes.

Prue quickly remembered a spell she'd glanced over in *The Book of Shadows*, a spell she'd never tried. "I'm looking for rose powder, violet powder, ash powder, and something called . . . pipeswa?" she fibbed. "Do you have those?"

Prue and her sisters were still becoming familiar with the huge volume their grandmother had left them. It was an endless task, since the book seemed to change every time they opened it.

"Sure—but it's pipsissewa, known to those of us who suffered through botany class as *Chimaphila umbellata*," Adrienne corrected. She climbed onto a stepladder and reached for a glass jar high on a shelf. She opened the jar and scooped some of the evergreen herbs into a small paper bag. "When you use this, you should crush it really fine and then mix it with the rest of your ingredients," she explained.

As Adrienne took down the jar of rose powder, the wind chimes on the door tinkled and a man in his late twenties walked in. Prue checked out his black shirt and tie and well-cut black wool pants. His blond hair was short and conservative, silver wire-rimmed glasses framed his hazel eyes, and he carried an expensive leather briefcase. Prue pegged him for a young CEO—especially after she heard a muted ringing and saw him pull the tiniest and most elegant cell phone she had ever seen out of his pocket. This guy had really expensive toys.

He glanced around the shop. His eyes met Prue's—and he blushed. Prue tried not to look amused, but she couldn't help wondering what he was doing there. He didn't look the Wiccan type.

"Can I help you?" Adrienne asked.

The man turned to her. "I need dried rose petals, linden flowers, bayberry, queen's root, and one of those little round black things you burn incense on," he blurted out in a rush.

"You mean charcoal," Adrienne said.

He nodded vigorously, his face beet red.

Adrienne's eyes met Prue's. It was clear to both of them that the guy wanted to do a love spell, and it was embarrassing him to death.

Adrienne's ash-blond brows drew together. "Are you *sure* you want to cast this spell?" she asked.

"Y-yes," the man stammered.

"Love spells can be very dangerous," she warned him. "Especially for beginners."

"How did you know I was casting a—"

"Those ingredients are very common in love spells," Adrienne replied. "Pretty standard stuff. But I have to warn you, magic is unpredictable. I cast a love spell once, and it worked. The guy I cast it on fell in love—with my roommate!"

Prue bit back a smile. She knew Adrienne was trying to keep this guy out of trouble—but she was also having a little fun with him while she was at it.

"She's right," Prue said, joining in the game.

She picked up one of the athames and tested its point against her fingertip. Adrienne's customer watched her intently. He seemed both fascinated and frightened. And he was *so* cute; it was a shame he already had a crush on someone else.

"I cast a love spell seven years ago," Prue lied. "And the guy fell in love with me just the way he was supposed to, but then I fell *out* of love, and he didn't."

"What happened to him?" the young man asked.

"Suicide," Prue intoned dramatically, her face grave. "I mean, I felt terrible about it, but once you cast a spell, it's not easy to reverse it." She shuddered and set down the athame.

Out of the corner of her eye, Prue saw Adrienne trying hard not to laugh as she measured out rose petals and queen's root.

Adrienne set the ingredients on the counter. "I had a love spell cast on me last year," she said. "My boyfriend put it on me while I was sleeping, and he must have said something about how our love would be uplifting, because for a week after I couldn't stop levitating."

"Le-levitating?" the man echoed. The young man was no longer red-faced. He'd gone chalk white. He stared at the ingredients Adrienne had set on the counter. "You know what?" he said. "I want to think about this some more."

"That's a good idea," Adrienne assured him. "You do that."

The man yanked open the door and ran from

the shop. "Ta-ta!" Prue called. "Come back again soon!" Then she and Adrienne burst out laughing. They laughed so hard, Prue had to grab the counter to steady herself. Adrienne wiped tears from her eyes.

"Was that too mean?" Adrienne asked, gasping for breath.

"I don't know, but it sure was fun," Prue said. "And he kind of deserved it. Love spells mean you're trying to use magic to control someone else—not exactly a healthy way to start a relationship."

Adrienne shook her head, smiling. "Well, I think we cured him. But telling him your boyfriend committed *suicide*? Wasn't that a little too dramatic?" She waggled a finger at Prue.

Prue grinned. "Well, maybe a little. But what about your levitating story. I mean, come on!"

Adrienne shrugged. "Okay, I was exaggerating. There was no boyfriend, no love spell. But one part *was* true." She hesitated. "Can I trust you with a secret?"

Prue met her eyes. "Of course you can."

"It's not something I got from a spell or incantation," Adrienne confessed. "But since I turned thirteen I really have been able to levitate."

Prue's mind reeled. Levitate? Could it be true? Could Adrienne have innate powers? That would make her another witch—a *true* witch like Prue and her sisters. "You mean that on your birthday—" she began.

Adrienne nodded. "On my birthday I discovered I had this power inside me. It took me time to control it, and for a while I thought my mom would flip out, but it's just something I realized I could do." She eyed Prue wistfully. "Did anything like that ever happen to *you?*"

There was a loneliness in Adrienne's voice that Prue recognized. It was a burden having these powers, she knew. And it was even more difficult keeping them to yourself all the time. It made her ache to tell Adrienne the truth. It would be such a relief to have someone to share her own story with, someone outside the family who wouldn't be all caught up in Halliwell history. . . .

No, she decided. She wasn't ready to open up—not yet. "I'm sorry, but nothing like that ever happened to me," she forced herself to say.

The chimes on the door rang, and three teenage girls bounded into the store. "We want to be witches," the shortest one announced. "Do you sell witch gear?"

Adrienne shot Prue a look of amused alarm.

The moment for personal revelations was past. "I'd better go," Prue said.

"I'll be with you three in a minute," Adrienne told the girls. She placed a slender hand on Prue's. "Wait here a second. Let me get you the rest of your ingredients." She quickly measured out some lavender powder and another white powder, then began to ring them up on the register.

Prue glanced at the white powder; it had a grainy quality that she recognized. "This isn't ash powder," she said. "It's hemlock."

Adrienne stared into the bag. "Omigosh—you're right! I can't believe I made such a ridiculous mistake. I am *so* sorry. Let me get you the ash powder." She found the correct ingredient, and as Prue paid at the cash register, Adrienne nodded in the direction of the three teens. *"Witch gear?"* she whispered.

Prue shrugged, barely joining in on the joke. As she left the shop a nagging thought troubled her. If she hadn't recognized the hemlock powder, if she'd taken it home and used it, it would have reversed her spell completely. She didn't even want to think about the damage that would have caused.

How could Adrienne have made such a basic mistake? she wondered. Could she have given me the wrong ingredient on purpose?

Prue pushed the thought from her mind. No, she scolded herself. You're being paranoid again. Your brain is just in shock because you finally met someone you can relate to. Adrienne is a friend. A friend who simply made a silly mistake.

CHAPTER
5

The next day at two, Piper drove up to the front of P3. Daria and Celeste were sitting in the backseat. "Here we are," Piper announced.

"This is it?" Daria did not sound impressed.

"The outside of the building's not fancy," Piper admitted, "but inside is a whole different story."

Celeste climbed out of the car and stared at the locked door. "So there's no one else inside now?"

"It's just going to be us," Piper said. She grabbed the bag of groceries that contained fresh ingredients, then fished the club keys out of her bag. "The staff doesn't come in until early evening, so we've got the place to ourselves."

She opened the metal grill gate and then the glass door, and the two girls filed in ahead of her. "The kitchen is straight back and then on your left," Piper called as she flicked the light switch. The club lit up with glittering lights and neon.

"Whoa!" the girls gasped. "This place is awesome!" Celeste observed.

"Thanks." Piper smiled at the compliment.

"Totally cool!" Daria leaped onto the stage and launched into playing intense air guitar. " 'I'm gonna take you away!' " she belted out, cheerfully off-key. Celeste joined her, holding an imaginary microphone and singing backup.

Piper walked over to the DJ booth and turned on the state-of-the-art sound system. She slipped a CD into the player and adjusted the volume.

" 'I wanna take you away!' " Bruce Smithe and the Rangers belted out over the club's huge speakers.

"Yeah! Awesome!" Daria called out. The girls continued to "perform" onstage, this time in sync with the music.

Meanwhile Piper decided to raid the refrigerator for the additional ingredients that they'd need. She went into the kitchen and dropped the bag of groceries onto the counter, smiling at the terrible crooning coming from the main room.

They're like any ordinary kids right now, she thought. Just having fun. And I'm helping them do that! She smiled and boogied over to the huge industrial-size refrigerator. As always, she glanced over at the temperature gauge before opening the door.

That's odd, Piper thought. The gauge was reading much higher than usual. She opened the door, expecting a blast of cold air to rush out at her as it always did. Instead—nothing.

Oh, no! No, no, no! Piper closed the refrigerator door. She moved to the counter at the far end of the room and paged through the phone book. She picked up the kitchen phone and dialed the number for the refrigerator-repair company, then explained the problem and gave them the club's address.

"We should be able to get to you in about four hours," the woman on the other end of the phone explained.

Four hours? Piper groaned as she hung up. She checked the contents of the refrigerator. Except for the eggs, everything else should be fine for four hours, she decided. But the freezer—she couldn't risk having all that meat and ice cream defrost and then not be able to be frozen again.

She debated for about ten seconds and then made the only decision she could. Her sisters were not going to like it, but they'd just have to deal.

Piper walked out to the main room. The two girls were still onstage, now singing a duet. When they noticed Piper watching them, they hammed it up, playing the rock star act to the hilt. They really were pretty adorable, she thought.

She waited till the song was done, dutifully applauded, then said, "We have a problem, and I'm going to need your help. The refrigerator's on the blink, so we're going to have to go to my house to stash the stuff from the freezer right away—before it goes bad. Will you two help me?"

"No problem," Daria said, jumping down from the stage.

Celeste tugged on the hem of her red T-shirt. "What about making pizza?"

"We'll make it at my house," Piper promised. "We don't have a special brick oven there, but we can still cook something totally delicious."

Piper and the girls went to work. With three sets of hands, the food transfer went quickly.

Half an hour later Piper pulled up in front of Halliwell Manor. She couldn't ignore an uneasy twinge of conscience. She had told her sisters she wouldn't bring Celeste to the house, and now she was breaking her promise—times two. Well, at least Prue's at work, she consoled herself. And hopefully, Phoebe is off practicing karate chops or something.

"This is where you live?" Celeste asked.

"You must be rich," Daria commented.

"It was our grandmother's house," Piper explained as they started unloading the car. "My sisters and I inherited it when she died. It's pretty funky inside."

"Are we going to meet your sisters?" Daria asked eagerly.

"Hope not," Piper replied under her breath. She handed each of the girls a bag, and then grabbed two more. "Follow me," she said, leading them up the steps. She felt a bit as though she was leading a troop of Girl Scouts.

Here goes, Piper thought as she balanced the bags and opened the door. She poked her head inside. The coast was clear—no Phoebe or Prue in sight. "Come on in," she told the girls. "The kitchen's off to the right."

"Wow!" Daria nearly banged into an end table as she gazed up at the stained glass windows. "It's like a church in here!"

Funny, somehow I don't think anyone would confuse us Halliwells with saints, Piper thought.

"Come on, guys," she called. "In here."

The girls followed her into the kitchen, and they set their bags down on the island. "Let's put all this stuff away," Piper told them. "And then I promise we'll make pizza."

Celeste opened the freezer. "Is it okay if I clear one of the shelves for the food from the club?"

"That's a terrific idea," Piper said, noticing that Celeste seemed a little more relaxed now that they were in the kitchen. Meanwhile Daria was . . . where *was* Daria?

Piper stuck her head out into the dining room and found Daria standing in front of a wall of framed sepia-toned photographs.

"Who *are* all these people?" Daria wanted to know.

"Distant relatives," Piper answered. "I don't even know most of their names."

"Aren't there any photos of you and your sisters?"

"Not on that wall," Piper said.

"So do your sisters look like you?"

"Sort of," Piper answered patiently. "We all have dark, straight hair. Come on, I need you in the kitchen."

Daria followed her into the kitchen, firing more questions at her. "Are you the youngest? What do your sisters do?"

"Daria, this isn't twenty questions," Piper said.

Daria giggled. "Sorry. I guess I'm just nosy."

Piper was pleased to see that Celeste had managed to fit all the club food into the freezer—almost.

She held up a container of ice cream. "I can't find any place to put this," she explained with a grin.

"That's okay," Piper assured her. "I know just how to take care of it." Piper opened a cupboard and pulled out two bowls and two spoons. She handed Celeste a spoon. "Go for it, gals. You've earned it."

While Celeste and Daria scarfed down their ice cream, Piper lit the oven and assembled the ingredients for the pizza. Was it possible, she wondered, for them to make pizza and get out of the house before Prue or Phoebe came home? She really, really hoped so.

Celeste put her bowl into the sink and joined Piper at the cutting board. "So—do we start with the dough, the sauce, or the toppings?"

"We're going to cheat and use dough I brought from the club. If we made it from scratch, we'd need a few hours for the dough to rise," Piper explained. "And I've got to get you two back to the Sunrise Center and me back to the club before five. So . . . let's make sauce."

Celeste immediately got to work. She smoothly moved back and forth between browning Italian sausage and chopping tomatoes. And Daria . . . Daria was going through the kitchen drawers.

"Are you looking for something?" Piper asked her.

"No, I just like to see what people have in their houses," Daria answered. "It tells you a lot about a person, you know? And I want to know all about you, Piper."

Piper steered Daria over to an empty counter. "Well, something I can tell you about me is that I like lots of garlic in my sauce, so why don't you start chopping some," she suggested.

"Okay," Daria said, but she didn't sound happy about it.

Piper emptied a paper bag of mushrooms into the colander and began to wash them off. She could see Celeste out of the corner of her eye. The girl seemed completely at home in the kitchen—draining the fat from the sausages, then adding the other ingredients in exactly the right order. She even seemed to know how much of each spice to add without measuring.

"Have you done this before?" Piper asked her.

"Not pizza, but I've made lots of spaghetti with tomato sauce," Celeste said. "In my last foster home, I used to do most of the KP. It was the only thing I liked about that place." She shrugged. "I always feel really content when I'm cooking."

"Me, too," Piper admitted. She gave Celeste a warm smile—a smile that Celeste actually returned. Score one for me, Piper thought. Too bad Daria didn't seem to be having as much fun. Piper turned to try to include her in the conversation—and discovered Daria had vanished. "*Now* where is she?" Piper muttered. She dried her hands on a dish towel and walked into the living room.

Daria was nowhere in sight. Piper hurried into the room their grandmother had called the conservatory. The wall of windows facing south, and plants covering nearly every surface gave it a summery feel. Nope, Daria was nowhere among the plants and white wicker furniture.

"Daria?" she called. When she got no reply, Piper climbed the stairs, hoping, *hoping* she'd find Daria on the second floor. She did a quick check of the bedrooms. They looked exactly as they'd been left that morning. And there was no sign of the young girl.

Piper's heart pounded. Her stomach began to churn. Daria couldn't have wandered all the way up to the attic, could she? The thought sent Piper running up the second flight of stairs.

The attic: where she and her sisters kept *The Book of Shadows*, the key to all their powers.

"Daria!" Piper called. Oh, please, don't let her be in there, she prayed. "Daria!" she called again.

"What?" Daria leaned over the wooden banister and gazed down at her.

Did she go into the attic? Piper wondered

frantically. Did she find the book? She tried to speak as calmly as she could, "You're supposed to be making pizza with me and Celeste. *In the kitchen.*"

Daria grinned at her. "I know. The truth is, cooking doesn't do much for me. But this house is *so* great—all these rooms and all this wild furniture." She gestured toward the attic's closed door. "What's in there?"

"A lot of dust," Piper answered between clenched teeth.

"Can I see?" Daria spun and reached for the doorknob.

"No!" Piper snapped. Daria turned around and stared at her suspiciously. Keep your cool, Piper, she told herself. This is a young girl—not a warlock or anything. She hasn't seen the book, so what are you worried about?

"Daria," she continued in a more reasonable tone. "I'm sorry, but if you want to be here, then you need to be in the kitchen with me and Celeste."

"Fine, if you're going to be that way about it." Daria narrowed her eyes at Piper. "Guess that just proves how much you trust me. Wouldn't want the halfway-house kid ripping off your precious photographs or—"

"Daria, that's not fair—" Piper began. But the words froze in her throat when she saw Prue standing at the bottom of the stairs.

"Hi, Piper." Prue was smiling, but Piper recognized that her sister's voice was tight with anger. "Who's your friend?"

"Wh-what are you doing home this early?" Piper asked.

"I've had a headache all day," Prue explained. "And I think it just got worse."

Daria bounced down the stairs. "Hi, I'm Daria," she said. "Which sister are you?"

Celeste chose that moment to emerge from the kitchen. "Hey," she said, sounding relieved. "I was wondering where everyone was."

"Everyone?" Prue echoed. "Just how many people are there in the house right now, Piper?"

"This is it," Piper assured her. "Counting you, just the four of us." The front door opened and Phoebe came in. "Oh, great. Here's one more." Piper wondered if Prue's headache was contagious. She could feel her temples throbbing.

Phoebe's eyes went from Piper, to Prue, to the girls, then back to Piper again. "What's going on?" she asked.

"Prue, Phoebe," Piper spoke quickly, "this is Daria and this is Celeste, my mentorees. We're making pizza. And we'd really better get back to the kitchen *right now*. We don't want that sauce to burn."

Piper hurried the two girls back to the kitchen, trying to figure out a way to get this day back on track. Okay. I'll finish the pizza, get the girls back to the Sunrise Center, and then I'll deal with Phoebe and Prue. She pushed a strand of hair out of her face. Or maybe I'll check into the Sunrise Center myself.

She stirred the sauce and was relieved to see that Celeste had already managed to get the dough rolled out and into the large round pizza pan. The point was to have fun with these girls and bond, she reminded herself. So bond.

"Toppings!" she sang out as cheerfully as she could. "Celeste, you're on green peppers. Daria, you chop mushrooms. Some fresh tomatoes would be good, too."

Prue stuck her head into the kitchen. "Piper, could I see you for a moment?" she asked sweetly. "Alone."

No doubt about it, Piper thought, I definitely caught Prue's headache. "One of you should keep stirring that sauce," she told the girls.

She followed Prue into the conservatory where Phoebe was waiting. Uh-oh, Piper thought. Phoebe looked almost as grim as Prue. Not a good sign.

"Piper, how could you bring those girls here when we agreed you wouldn't?" Prue asked in a furious whisper. "What were you thinking?"

"And how did you wind up with *two* mentorees?" Phoebe added.

"One question at a time," Piper said, holding up a hand. She gave her sisters the short version of how Daria and Celeste wound up cooking there. "So I really had no choice," she finished. "I promised them a cooking date, and we had to come here anyway to store the frozen food—"

"I don't believe this," Prue said.

"It was a crazy thing to do," Phoebe agreed. "Besides, if you couldn't cook at the club, why didn't you just tell them you'd cook some other time and—I don't know—take them to the zoo instead?"

"The zoo?" Piper rubbed her temples. "They're thirteen, not five!"

"When I came in, Daria was on the stairs," Prue reminded her. "Please tell me she wasn't in the attic."

"No, I caught her before she got that far," Piper replied.

"Bringing them here isn't even the worst of it," Prue went on. "Someone was watching us at the club the other night, remember? What if trouble is brewing? What if a warlock or something *is* after us? Do you really want to put these girls in danger? Do you want to be responsible for their safety?"

Piper knew Prue had a point, but she refused to allow her older sister to dissuade her. Being a witch wasn't going to completely control her life. And she'd never let anything bad happen to Celeste or Daria. "This is important to me," Piper declared. "And these girls need me. I can't just walk away from them."

"Piper, I know you mean well, but you really need to rethink this," Phoebe said gently.

"Look, I'll admit that they're a handful," Piper said. "Especially Daria. But—" Piper broke off when she became aware of a movement behind her.

She turned around and found Daria staring at her, a steely look in her eyes.

Prue and Phoebe gasped. Piper felt sick with panic. She knew her sisters were wondering the same thing she was. How long had Daria been standing there? How much had she heard?

CHAPTER

6

Daria," Piper finally found her voice to ask, "how much of this conversation have you been listening to?"

"Enough," Daria snapped. "Enough to know that you don't care about me. Your sisters don't even want me in your house." She darted around Piper toward the door. Prue and Phoebe instinctively backed up to let her pass.

"Daria, wait," Piper protested. "That's not true! I *do* care. I care about you a lot." She dashed up to the girl and placed a hand on her arm.

"Don't touch me," Daria ordered, her eyes blazing with anger. "I don't stay where I'm not wanted. I had enough of that in foster homes."

Piper recoiled as if she'd been slapped. How had she managed to blow things so completely?

The last thing she wanted to do was make Daria feel like an unwanted foster kid again.

"I'm sorry," Piper apologized. "I'm sorry if anything we said hurt you. Please come back inside and give me a chance to explain."

"You are such a liar," Daria scoffed. "A big phony. Why can't you admit it? Celeste is the one you like. You only agreed to take me on because you thought it would make Celeste happy. So, fine. You two can play Harriet Homemaker together. And I promise not to bother you anymore." Daria flung open the front door, bolted down the stairs, and up the street. Piper stared helplessly after her.

"What's going on?" Piper heard someone behind her ask. She turned to see Celeste standing by the kitchen, her eyes darting from one sister to another. Confusion played across her pale features. "Where's Daria?"

"Daria just left," Piper said.

Celeste's eyes widened in surprise. "Why?"

"I'll explain later," Piper said. She reached for her car keys. "Right now I need you to help me find her. And, Phoebe, do me a big favor and turn off the sauce on the stove."

"Whatever you say," Phoebe replied. She spun on her heel and charged into the kitchen.

Prue crossed her arms in front of her. "Piper, we still have to—"

"Stop. Okay, Prue? Just save it," Piper cut her off. She massaged her pounding head. "We'll talk later," she promised. "At this second it is way more important that I find Daria." She turned to Celeste. "Come on."

The fog was rolling in from the bay as Piper and Celeste drove through the narrow, residential streets. Piper had lived in San Francisco all her life but she was still always amazed by how quickly the city could be shrouded in mist. She turned on her headlights and leaned forward to peer through the windshield.

"I don't get it," Piper said, downshifting as she climbed another of San Francisco's nearly vertical hills. "How could Daria just vanish? She didn't have that much of a head start on us." Piper racked her brain, trying to think of where a ticked-off teenager might go to cool down. "Does Daria have any places in the city that she particularly likes?" she asked Celeste. "A favorite store or park or video arcade?"

Celeste gazed out the side window. "Not that I know of. Maybe she went into a movie theater."

"Or maybe she's hiding behind someone's garage or she got on a bus." Piper smacked the steering wheel in frustration. "I shouldn't have hesitated for even a second. I should have gone right after her."

Actually, what she should have done was stop time as soon as Daria reached for the door. And she would have, if she hadn't been so afraid that one of the girls might somehow realize what was going on and discover the truth.

Maybe Prue was right, Piper thought. Maybe a

witch has no business being a mentor. She had certainly messed things up royally so far.

Piper would never be able to live with herself if anything happened to Daria. And what was she going to say to Mr. Morgan when she took Celeste back? That she'd lost the other kid she was supposed to be mentoring?

"Why did she bail?" Celeste's question broke through Piper's silent guiltfest.

"Because—" Piper slowed the car even further as the fog thickened. It was like driving through wads of gray cotton. "This is ridiculous," Piper muttered. "How can we be searching for someone when the visibility is all of two feet?"

"Piper, why did Daria run out?" Celeste persisted.

Piper decided Celeste deserved the truth. "Daria overheard me talking with my sisters," Piper explained. "And she misunderstood some of the things we said. She thought I didn't care about her. But I do. I care about both of you very much."

"Your sisters didn't want us there," Celeste said in a quiet voice. "I could tell when I saw their faces. Especially Prue."

Piper thought about denying it, but Daria already thought she was liar; she didn't want to lose Celeste's trust, too.

"My sisters have their reasons," Piper answered at last. "You're just going to have to trust me when I tell you that those reasons have nothing to do with you or Daria."

"What is it then?"

"Family stuff," Piper replied. "Old, complicated family stuff. I can't talk about it any more than that—except to say that it doesn't affect the way I feel about either of you girls."

Piper pulled to a stop at a red light. She had reached the edge of the Mission District now—not exactly San Francisco's safest neighborhood. "Do you think Daria might have gone this way?" Piper asked.

"Do you have a cell phone?" Celeste wondered.

"Yeah, why?"

"Why don't you try the Sunrise Center and see if she went back there?"

Piper covered her forehead with her hand. She was so frantic, she hadn't even thought of that. "Good idea." Piper pulled out her cell phone just as the light changed to green. She handed the phone to Celeste. "Why don't you make the call?"

"Sure." Celeste punched in the numbers, and when someone answered the phone, she asked for Daria. A moment later Piper heard her say, "Hey, Daria, you okay?" She listened to Daria's response, then told Piper, "She's fine."

Piper held out her hand for the phone. "Can I talk to her?" Celeste gave her the phone. "Daria, it's Piper. Are you all right?"

"Why should you care?" Daria snarled.

She's fine, Piper decided. Angry, but fine. She turned a corner, heading toward the halfway house. "Daria," Piper said into the phone. "I'm really sorry about what happened."

"Not sorry enough." With a click, the phone went dead.

Ookay . . . Piper folded up the phone. "Great conversation," she reported. "I feel like we really bonded there."

"Daria can be a little moody," Celeste admitted.

"A little?"

"She's just been hurt a lot. She doesn't want to get hurt again."

"I know," Piper said with a sigh. She'd find a way to mend things with Daria. She had to. And then she had to find out how much, if anything, Daria knew about her and her sisters. If she didn't find out for sure, they'd be too vulnerable.

On Saturday afternoon Phoebe inched her way up into the crowded bleachers of the Oakland stadium. She was impressed by the huge turnout for the Bay Area Martial Arts Meet. She'd found out that the tournament lasted the entire weekend, with events for kids, adults, and even seniors. There were board-breaking demonstrations, and competitions in kata, self-defense, and weapons technique. Of course, none of those events were what she was there to see.

Phoebe found a seat, then flipped open her program. "Intermediate-level sparring," she murmured. She ran her finger along the names until she found the one she was looking for—Kenji

Yamada. Kenji's match was scheduled to begin at two-fifteen. She glanced at her watch. It was two o'clock now, so he should be here somewhere.

She peered down at the benches that lined the ring. She spotted Kenji sitting among the competitors, looking handsome in a spotless white gi. He was wearing his brown belt from his old school, which made sense. It wouldn't be fair if he fought a beginner. Sensei Towers paced in front of the benches.

Kenji looked a little nervous. Phoebe smiled smugly. If he knew what I knew, she thought, remembering her premonition, he'd know he had nothing to worry about.

Phoebe studied the two fighters in the ring— two teenage girls wearing green belts. She admired their sharp, clean technique. Hey, I must be learning something, Phoebe realized. I can recognize the moves!

A bell sounded, the girls bowed to each other, and one of them was declared the winner and received a trophy.

"We'll now begin men's intermediate karate *kumite*," the M.C. announced. *Kumite*, Phoebe had learned, was Japanese for fighting.

Phoebe's heart sped up a little as Kenji stepped into the ring. His opponent was another brown belt, a tall guy with sun-bleached reddish hair, who gave off surfer vibes.

Kenji and his opponent bowed to each other, then took fighting stances.

"Hajime!" the referee called out, and the match began.

Phoebe watched as Kenji's opponent began with a flurry of punches and kicks, including a side kick that looked powerful enough to send a cow flying. Kenji avoided them all, blocking, dodging, slipping out of the way, never actually making contact. Then the red-haired guy threw an upper cut, and Kenji delivered a powerful punch to his opponent's solar plexus. He quickly followed it with a roundhouse kick that finished it. Two simple strikes and the surfer dude folded.

Ow! Phoebe winced as Kenji's opponent went down. It was a little strange to watch the guy she had a crush on look so lethal.

Kenji was declared winner of the match. That meant he would fight the winner of the next round. Phoebe wondered how many matches Kenji would have to fight before the scene in her vision came true.

All in all, Phoebe watched Kenji fight four fights and win three of them. In the fourth fight he was up against a guy who looked like he pumped iron big time—the jacket of his gi barely closed over his pecs. He didn't have Kenji's elegant form, but he had power. And Kenji was clearly tiring. A wicked roundhouse kick to the jaw seemed to throw him. After that his rhythm was off, his movements slower. Phoebe could tell he was struggling just to stay in the ring.

The fight ended, and Phoebe let out a sigh of relief. The referee held up Kenji's hand. "Kenji

Yamada, second place," the official announced. It all played out exactly as she'd seen in the vision. A tiny shiver tingled along her spine. No matter how many times it happened, her ability to see the future still unnerved her a little.

A black belt handed Kenji a trophy. Phoebe applauded loudly, and threw in a wolf-whistle for good measure. As the first-place winner received his trophy, she made her way down to the floor. She intercepted Kenji on his way to the men's locker room.

"Phoebe, you came after all!" Kenji looked pleased.

"I got out of my commitment," she said. Actually, she hadn't. She'd left a note for Prue, hoping her big sister would understand. "You were incredible!" she told Kenji.

"Not in that last fight," he admitted, rubbing his bruised jaw. "But it felt good to make it to the final round. I did better than I expected, especially considering how long it's been since the last time I fought." He gazed at her. "Funny. I took second place. It was exactly as you predicted."

Phoebe smiled. "Lucky guess."

"Uh-huh," Kenji eyed her warily. "Sure it was."

Phoebe smiled her most seductive smile at him. "I also predicted that you'd be so caught up in the tournament that you wouldn't even notice I was here."

"Well, that's one prediction that couldn't possibly come true," Kenji observed. His warm eyes crinkled at her. "But it's a good thing I didn't know you were here. It would have been far too distracting. I wouldn't have been able to keep my mind on the match."

"Oh, really," Phoebe responded, moving closer to him. "What would you have been thinking about?"

Kenji put his hands on her waist. "I would have been wondering what it's like to kiss you."

Phoebe placed her hand on his shoulder and lifted her face to his. "I think we could answer that question right now."

His lips met hers—hesitantly at first. There was something gentle in Kenji that Phoebe found completely adorable. She let him know that there was no reason to hesitate. He drew her close and the kiss deepened. Phoebe pressed her body against his, forgetting everyone and everything around her—giving herself over to Kenji's intensity.

Finally she pulled away. "Wow," she murmured. She took a tiny step back but stayed wrapped in his arms. She felt safe and happy in his embrace.

Kenji gazed at her, his eyes lit with desire. "*That* was incredible," he said at last.

Phoebe nodded and tried not to look as goofy and happy as she felt. How often did she luck into this kind of connection with a guy as sweet as Kenji?

"I think we have to do that again," Kenji whispered in her ear. "So I can convince myself I'm not imagining things."

He pulled her to him again, and Phoebe felt her more practical side surface. Be careful, she told herself. You're falling way too fast for this guy. Slow it down.

Kenji sensed her hesitation. "Don't try to resist, Phoebe," he chided her softly. With one hand he gently lifted her face to meet his. "I've got you now."

CHAPTER
7

When the coven met again that night, the Master was seething.

"We still have not discovered the powers of the Charmed Ones! What has taken so long? Must one of us be destroyed by their power before we strike?"

No one dared answer him.

"Their powers," he repeated. "We must find a way to leech them, invert them, weaken them." His voice rose to a thundering roar. "You have all failed! And for failure, there is a price!"

He waved his hands over the crowd. Each coven member doubled over. They moaned and writhed in pain. After a few moments the Master gestured again. The wailing ceased.

"We cannot afford failure," the Master whispered. "Do I make myself clear?"

"Yes, Master," the group chanted.

"Very well then."

He pulled an object from beneath his robe. A red satin ribbon with a knot tied in the middle. "We will call on the power of our talisman to aid us, but everyone's continued diligence is crucial to the mission." He paused. "Adrienne, step forward."

The blond-haired woman moved toward the altar.

"Tell me, my chosen spider, what is your plan for defeating the Charmed Ones?"

"I-I'm going to win the trust of a Charmed one, find out what her and her sisters' powers are, then turn them against them," she answered.

"There's hope for you yet," the Master declared dryly. "And you, Kenji?"

"I'm going to make the youngest sister fall in love with me," he answered. "I'm going to take her heart. And then I'm going to destroy it."

The next afternoon, before the club opened, Piper sat on one of the barstools, studying a computer printout of recent orders.

"Any fascinating conclusions?" Pete, the bartender, asked.

"Profits are through the roof. Maybe we should extend our hours. You know, open earlier, close later?" Piper reported. "Maybe we ought to open during lunch as a café."

"Think that's our first customer?" Pete asked, tilting his head toward the entrance.

Piper spun around on the barstool and saw Phoebe standing just inside the door. She looked uncharacteristically nervous, Piper observed.

"Another surprise visit?" Piper said. "Hooked on being my cleanup crew?"

"No, I need to talk to you," Phoebe said, peeling off her jacket.

"Speak."

Phoebe glanced at Pete. "Alone," she muttered.

Piper led Phoebe to a table, hoping that her sister wasn't about to inform her that some demon had walked into their lives, threatening to exterminate them or something.

"I meant to tell you this last night, but I guess I chickened out," Phoebe confessed.

"Go on," Piper's hands tensely gripped the seat of her chair.

"I met someone last week," Phoebe blurted out. "A male someone."

Piper felt herself relax. This kind of problem— the human kind—she could deal with. "Really?"

Phoebe nodded. "A gorgeous, charming, nice, intelligent, sexy, male someone."

Piper smiled. "What's his name?"

"Kenji Yamada. He's in my karate class. He moved up here from San Diego to do grad work at Berkeley. He's an engineer."

"Wow! He sounds amazing," Piper said, trying to be encouraging. "Have you mentioned this model citizen to Prue?"

Phoebe winced. "No, I'm not ready for the we-have-to-be-careful-about-who-we-let-into-our-lives lecture yet, thank you." She paused. "You know, the sad thing is, Prue would probably like him, but she'd still give me the family speech. She can't help herself."

"Well, there *are* certain drawbacks to dating when you're a you-know-what," Piper admitted.

"Agreed." Phoebe dropped her head in her arms. "That's why this whole thing is making me extremely nervous."

"Because?"

"Because of everything," Phoebe wailed. She lifted her head. "Because of the family stuff and how weird it will be if I ever have to tell him what I am. Because I never know when some warlock is going to pop out of the woodwork. But mostly because I really, really don't want to wreck this."

Piper studied her younger sister curiously. When it came to guys, Phoebe was usually a free spirit. Piper had never heard her sound so serious about a relationship before. Especially after knowing the guy for only one week!

Phoebe straightened up in her chair. "I want to take this one slow," she said.

It was all Piper could do to keep her jaw from dropping open. Slow? Phoebe? This guy really must be different.

"Well?" Phoebe demanded. "Aren't you going to tell me that's an excellent, sane, and mature idea?"

Piper smiled. "It's an excellent, sane, and

mature idea, but—no offense—it doesn't sound like you."

"I know," Phoebe said. "I think it's just that I like Kenji so much."

"Then go for it—" Piper began. She stopped talking as she realized that Celeste was peering in at them through the window. The girl was wearing a T-shirt and jeans, looking half-frozen and wholly miserable. Alarms went off in Piper's head. *What is Celeste doing here? Something must be wrong.*

She gestured for the girl to come in. "I'm afraid I'm going to have to cut this short," Piper told Phoebe apologetically.

"It's okay," Phoebe said. "We covered the essentials. I just had to tell someone."

Celeste stepped into the club, and Piper waved her over to the table. "Hi, Celeste," she said. "You remember my sister Phoebe?"

"I remember." Celeste's voice was cool and wary.

Phoebe smiled at the girl. "I'm sorry things were tense when you were at the house. And I've got to run now, but maybe we can all get together soon and get to know one another."

Celeste looked surprised. "Sure," she said. "That would be great."

After Phoebe left, Celeste said, "Hey, she's nice!"

"Yeah, she's pretty decent," Piper agreed with a grin. Then her forehead wrinkled with concern. "Are you all right?"

Celeste nodded, but Piper wasn't convinced. "You look like you're about two degrees away from frostbite. Let me get you some hot tea. Do you want to borrow a sweater?"

Celeste shook her head impatiently. "Listen, it's Daria. She's been acting weird ever since that blowup at your house on Friday."

"Sit," Piper ordered. She brought Celeste a cup of hot mint tea. "So," she said, sitting down across from the girl. "Tell me what's going on."

"Daria sneaked out the last two nights. Both times she didn't come back in until three or four in the morning."

"Where does she go?" Piper asked.

"I don't know. She isn't talking to me. Or anyone at the center. Except to make weird threats. They're really freaking me out."

"What do you mean, threats?" Piper asked, growing more concerned.

"Things like, 'No one cares about me now, but they will—afterward.' Yesterday I caught her standing in front of the mirror, murmuring, 'Soon they'll all disappear.' "

Celeste's eyes flicked to Piper's face as if she were trying to gauge Piper's reaction. Piper kept her expression neutral, trying to give the impression that she handled problems like this all the time. But inside, Piper's heart thumped against her rib cage. This did not sound good at all.

Celeste shifted in her seat and stared down at

her hands. Piper wondered if Celeste felt as if she was snitching on Daria. "It's okay, Celeste," Piper assured her. "It's important that you tell me everything."

Celeste took in a breath. "Today was the strangest. She said something like, 'Soon I'll call up the darkness.'"

Piper's head snapped up. Call up the darkness? That sounded like an incantation.

"Have you told Mr. Morgan about this?" Piper asked.

Celeste snorted. "Yeah, right. He'd just say it was nothing to worry about." She leaned across the table. "I thought it would be better if I came to you."

Piper felt her heart going out to the girl. It was obvious now—Celeste really trusted her.

"Daria's scaring me," Celeste continued. "I think she's gotten into some freaky stuff. Will you talk to her?"

Piper stood up and got her jacket and a spare sweater for Celeste. "Pete, I'll be back as soon as I can."

"By the time we open?"

"I'll try," Piper promised. "This is an emergency."

Piper and Celeste climbed into her car, then Piper headed for the Sunrise Center. It was another chilly, gloomy day, the sky low and ominous.

"Was Daria at the center when you left to find me?" Piper asked.

"Yeah, that's when she was going on about calling up the darkness." Celeste's pale blue eyes studied Piper. "Why did you get so upset when you heard that?"

"I'm just worried about her," Piper answered. She didn't tell the girl exactly what she was beginning to suspect—that maybe Daria was becoming involved in black magic.

The more she learned about practitioners of the dark arts, the more they frightened her. They lured their followers in with promises of infinite power—and Piper knew that could be seductive, especially to kids like Daria who had next to nothing of their own, and no control over their own destinies. For once, Piper prayed that her suspicion was completely off the mark.

A few minutes later Piper parked across the street from the center. Mr. Morgan met them in the hallway of the building. "Celeste, thank goodness, you're back!"

Celeste scowled. "I didn't go very far."

"You know the rules," Mr. Morgan told her. "If you go out, you have to sign out, and let us know where you'll be and when you'll be back."

"She was with me," Piper said quickly. "I'm sorry, we forgot to sign out. Have you seen Daria?"

"She was upstairs just half an hour ago," Mr. Morgan answered.

"Do you mind if we go talk to her?"

"Absolutely not." Mr. Morgan smiled. "I'm glad to see how involved you've become in the mentoring program, Piper."

Piper gave him a quick smile and charged up the stairs. Celeste threw open the door to the dim little room. "She's gone," she announced. "I told you Morgan wouldn't even notice."

"Then we'll wait for her." Celeste sprawled on her bunk and Piper paced the tiny room. *I'm probably way overreacting,* Piper thought. *Maybe Daria's just in a funk. Maybe there's no witchcraft involved here at all.* "Could Daria have gone to visit a friend?" Piper asked.

Celeste picked at the ripped knee of her jeans. "I don't think she has other friends." She paused. "I did hear her on the phone yesterday, though. She was talking to someone about a meeting. Then she said something about a master."

Piper leaned against the desk. "Master of what?"

Celeste shrugged. "I don't know. Maybe she was talking about that rap star, Master D."

Or a master of black magic, Piper thought with dismay.

That's it. It's definitely time to do a little investigating, if only to convince myself that I'm wrong about this, she decided. She had to risk it, for Daria's sake. She raised her hands and froze time—and Celeste. She crossed the room and locked the door. She worked quickly, all too aware that the length of her time-freezes could be unpredictable.

She tackled the dresser drawers first. The first two only held clothes, some of which she recognized as Celeste's. But in the third drawer, under Daria's red T-shirt, she found two thick black candles, a pentagram, and a crudely made doll.

Piper sat back on her heels. She let the evidence sink in. It looked as if Daria was dabbling in black magic. But how deep in was she?

Piper continued her search, worrying about what else she'd find. The fourth drawer held socks and underwear, and the closet revealed nothing more exciting than a few pieces of clothing, two small, empty suitcases, a bathrobe, and two thin coats.

Piper darted a quick glance at Celeste. Good. She was still frozen. She closed the closet door and quickly riffled through the desk drawers. Pencils, pens, a roll of tape, some envelopes, a blank notepad. And a neatly folded piece of red paper.

Piper unfolded the paper. There was an address scrawled on it: 4829 Colwood Street. She didn't know where it was, but maybe it was a clue to Daria's whereabouts.

A tiny flutter of movement caught her attention. The time-freeze was about to wear off. Piper quickly unlocked the door to the room and perched back on the desk.

"Piper?" Celeste blinked and looked at her in confusion. "I must have spaced out. What were you saying?"

Piper showed her the paper. "Is this Daria's handwriting?"

"Yes."

"Do you recognize the address?"

Celeste shook her head. "Nope."

"Well, I think we'd better check it out," Piper decided. "Now."

CHAPTER
8

Piper sat in the front seat of her car, peering at a map of the city.

"Did you find it?" Celeste asked eagerly.

"I think so." Piper's tone was grim. "This place, whatever it is, is not in the greatest neighborhood."

Actually that was a total understatement. Colwood Street was in the Western Addition. In the middle of the city, bordered by Hayes Valley and Fillmore, the Western Addition was one of the city's roughest neighborhoods. Just the other night on the news, Piper had seen a report of drive-by shootings in its projects and abandoned houses.

So what was Daria doing with this address? Piper wondered. Maybe she was involved with drugs or a gang. Piper shuddered. Both would be equally dangerous as fooling with black magic.

"What makes you so sure that Daria's at this address?" Celeste asked as they drove toward Fillmore.

"I'm not," Piper admitted. "But something is wrong with Daria. And if we want to find out what it is, right now this address is the only thing we've got to go on."

Patience, Piper told herself as she made her way down Fillmore Street by fits and starts. She would have willingly risked a speeding ticket, but the traffic was too thick to go much faster than twenty-five.

The cars thinned out as they reached Colwood. There were no projects along this street, Piper noted, only a burned-out collection of boarded-up buildings and vacant lots filled with garbage. Was Daria hiding out here? Piper drove even more slowly. She eyed a stained mattress, two ripped-out toilets, shattered dishes, a broken tricycle—nothing that seemed like it could shelter a runaway teen.

There was something about this street—something beyond the obvious filth and decay—that made Piper uneasy. She hoped they'd be able to find Daria quickly and get out of there.

"Do you see any street numbers?" she asked Celeste.

"They're not exactly easy to find on burned-out buildings," Celeste pointed out.

"I know, but look for forty-eight twenty-nine anyway."

Celeste shuddered. "Piper, I don't think I like this place."

"Me either," Piper admitted. She realized that Colwood Street was completely and utterly deserted. In other rough sections of the city, you'd at least see the occasional street person or a stray cat. But Colwood had a stillness about it that was terrifying. There were no signs of life on it at all.

Sweat trickled down Piper's back, and a chill ran through her. Suddenly, she had an awful taste in her mouth, and her stomach felt strange. Ugh. What was happening? Was she coming down with something?

"Do you think we should call out Daria's name?" Celeste asked nervously.

Piper shrugged, not trusting herself to speak. She didn't want to frighten Celeste by revealing how awful she felt. Or how much this place scared her.

"There!" Celeste cried. She pointed to the other side of the street where the ground sloped up toward the remains of a crumbling Victorian. Sure enough, the number 4829 was still visible on the front of the house.

Piper pulled up to the curb and studied the dark, gloomy structure. The roof was caving in on the third floor. The front of the house had been spray-painted long ago with gang graffiti, but even that was faded now. The windows were boarded up.

Piper's breath caught. The front door was ajar. Was Daria inside?

"This is it," Celeste said, scrambling out of the car.

Another chill shook Piper. Her stomach lurched. She felt sour bile rising in her throat. Is this food poisoning? She'd never felt so bad so fast. "Celeste, wait!" she called.

But Celeste was already walking toward the house.

Piper lay her forehead on the steering wheel. She felt in no condition to go chasing after Celeste. But she had no choice.

She slid out of the car and steadied herself against the door. Dusk was falling and the air was murky and heavy with the stench of rotting garbage. A wave of dizziness washed over her. Her stomach heaved, but she forced herself toward the house, where Celeste was picking her way up broken wooden stairs.

"Wait!" she shouted. But her shout barely carried. Instead, Celeste called, "Hey! The door is open!" She disappeared inside.

"No!" Piper cried. "Celeste, come back out here!"

Piper swayed, took a step forward, and another wave of nausea hit her. She seemed to grow worse the closer she drew to the house. This is no flu, Piper realized with growing fear. It was something generated by the house. And Celeste had just walked straight into the heart of it.

"Help!" Celeste's terrified scream pierced the thick air. "Piper, help me!"

Piper forgot about the sick feeling in her stomach. She struggled up the stairs and pushed open the rotting front door.

The inside of the house was pitch-dark. Piper blinked frantically, trying to will her eyes to adjust. "Celeste!" she cried out. "Where are you?"

"Up he—" The girl's cry broke off. But it was enough for Piper to realize that it came from above her.

She strained to see in the dark, and reaching out, found a wooden banister. Hold on, Celeste, she prayed silently. I'm almost there.

Nearly crawling, Piper dragged herself up the stairs. She gasped and stopped when she saw an eerie green glow on the landing above her. The hair on the back of her neck tingled with fear.

She forced her body up several more stairs, straining against her illness. You're almost there, she urged herself. Clutching the railing, she raised her head to see the landing. Celeste lay on the floor bathed in the eerie green light. Her arms were outstretched, her legs pressed together. As far as Piper could tell there was nothing binding the girl.

Nothing except black magic.

Piper crawled up the last step. It creaked beneath her weight and Celeste turned frantic eyes to her.

"Piper," she whimpered.

Before Piper could move another inch, a figure in a hooded black robe moved out of the shadows. He stepped into the green light. Piper couldn't see his face, but her eyes were riveted on the athame, a ceremonial dagger he clutched. He lifted it high above Celeste and in a vicious motion drove it down.

"No!" Piper screamed, using all her strength to raise her arms and freeze time. The dagger stopped in midair, just a foot from the girl's abdomen. Celeste froze, too, her eyes squeezed shut in fear.

We have to get out of here! Piper stumbled over to Celeste and tugged her hand, but as she suspected, Celeste was still bound by the warlock's magic. Piper couldn't budge her. Piper ran through the spells she'd been studying from *The Book of Shadows*. She hit on one she hoped would work:

> Loosen knots, dark magic unbind,
> Free the one whose heart is tied to mine.

She grabbed Celeste's hand again. Yes! This time it moved easily. I did it! Piper thought with relief. I dissolved the warlock's binding. The next problem was, Celeste was frozen along with the warlock and Piper was too weak to carry her out. She needed Celeste alert and awake, able to leave the house under her own power.

If she waited, the time-freeze spell would wear off. Celeste would be fine—but so would the warlock.

I need another spell, Piper thought frantically. But *what*?

Then it came to her—not a spell for Celeste, but one for the warlock. For insurance, she took the dagger from his stiffened fingers. Crossing her fingers for luck, she pointed the athame at the warlock and chanted:

Green as grass, green as the ocean's curl,
Light become web and bind he who'd harm
 the girl.
Green is the light, green shall it bend,
Bind this warlock and hold till time's end.

Piper held her breath as the green light brightened, then spun itself into long, slender strands. Within seconds they'd wrapped around the warlock, circling him, tightening, until he was swathed in a glowing green net.

Piper felt her knees buckling. But the spells had taken almost all the energy she had left. She felt the familiar stirring of the time-freeze fading. "Come on, Celeste," she murmured. "I can't carry you."

Celeste's eyes popped open. She stared at the warlock, who had also unfrozen and was struggling furiously against his bands. "Wh-what happened?" she asked Piper.

"Never mind that. We've got to get out of here—now!"

Piper turned and stumbled as she started down the dark stairway. She felt Celeste grasp her arm. "Come on. Lean on me," Celeste said.

Step by agonizing step, Celeste helped Piper down the stairs and out the door. Piper could feel a bit of her strength returning as they got farther from the house.

Piper slid into the driver's seat and put the key into the ignition. As they drove down the block, her strength returned.

Piper darted a sideways glance at Celeste. Her entire body was trembling violently.

Piper reached out and grasped her hand, then drove until they were well away from the Western Addition. She finally stopped at a fast-food restaurant.

"How about a milk shake?" she offered.

Celeste nodded, but instead of climbing out of the car, she threw her arms around Piper. "I was so scared," she cried.

Piper's heart went out to her. She sounded more like a kid than ever, like a lost, frightened little girl.

"I know." Piper held her and stroked her hair. "But it's over now. And you don't have to be afraid anymore. Because I'll protect you. I promise."

Celeste wiped her eyes. "Do you think Daria's in that house?"

"I hope not," Piper answered. Despite what she'd told Celeste, she was frightened. Whether Daria was in that house or not, she knew in her bones that this episode was far from over. She'd stopped one warlock, but the evil in that house was overwhelmingly strong. She was certain there were other warlocks there. They'd wanted her and they'd wanted Celeste. And in Piper's experience, warlocks didn't give up easily.

As they walked toward the restaurant, Piper

put her keys in her pocket—and felt the slip of paper with the Colwood Street address there.

The address that Daria had written down. She and Celeste had almost lost their lives, and it all traced back to Daria.

Piper shuddered. What kind of magic had the girl gotten herself mixed up in?

CHAPTER 9

Again it was night, and the coven had gathered. The Master placed several red ribbons in front of him. "The Charmed Ones are getting too close," he proclaimed. "They have defeated one of our brothers! He has been magically bound and cannot be freed."

A frightened murmur rippled through the crowd.

"Fear not. We must redouble our efforts," the Master insisted. He took hold of a chalice filled with blood. He sprinkled a few drops onto each of the ribbons.

He held the ribbons up to the crowd. "Now they will be no match for us!"

"Prue, I'm so glad you dropped by!" Adrienne greeted her from behind the counter. Her long lavender dress, with tiny beads sewn onto the quilted bodice, made Prue think her friend looked like a princess in a fairy tale. "I just got a shipment from a new botanicals company that you're not going to believe!"

"I swear, walking into this shop is dangerous," Prue joked.

Adrienne stopped short. "Wh-what do you mean?" she asked.

"You've always got some incredible find that I can't live without," Prue explained.

Adrienne smiled. "Then you're in extreme danger today," she said. "Look at this." She extracted a long, polished wooden chest from the shelf behind her. "True treasure," she crooned as she lifted the lid.

Prue saw that the inside of the box had been lined with dark blue velvet. Nestled snugly within the velvet were dozens of tiny blue glass bottles, each bearing a handwritten label.

Prue fingered the delicate bottles. "Stinging nettle, rock rose, yellow dock, greyana, false unicorn, horsetail, comfrey, bergamot, fenugreek, liferoot, valerian, mugwort, scullcap . . ." Prue read aloud. "What is all this stuff?"

"Tinctures and oils, most of which I've been trying to track down for ages." She sighed. "I finally feel that this store has everything that any Wiccan could want."

"I've felt that way since the first time I walked in here." Prue studied the tinctures. "Could I buy the liferoot from you?"

"So much for the complete collection." Adrienne

lifted the blue glass bottle out of the case and wrapped it in tissue paper.

"Prue," she said, "can I ask you something—as a friend?"

Prue smiled. She felt a happy warmth spread through her. Adrienne considered her a friend! "Sure," she told her.

"Do you remember what we were talking about the last time you were here? Right before the arrival of the teen brigade?"

"You mean, about your innate powers?" Prue asked, intrigued. She'd been hoping Adrienne would mention them again.

Adrienne handed Prue her tincture, then closed the wooden chest and put it back onto the shelf. "I told you that when I was a teenager I discovered I could levitate," she said. "Lately, I've been trying to cultivate another power. It's something I find I'm able to do—sometimes."

Prue leaned against the counter. "What kind of power are you talking about?"

Adrienne's voice dropped down to a whisper. "Telekinesis."

Prue felt a thrill of excitement. Was there another white witch with the same power that she had? She glanced at her watch. She only had a few minutes before an appointment, but she had to see this. "I can't stay long, but could you show me?"

"I'll try," Adrienne said. "I'm still a novice at this, so I can't promise it will work. I'll start with"—she set an amethyst crystal on the counter—"that."

Adrienne stared at the piece of purple quartz. Prue could feel her summoning energy, focusing it, and then directing it toward the rock. The amethyst didn't move at all.

Adrienne took a deep breath. Now Prue could sense her going deeper into herself, calling up power from the ground beneath them, using her body to concentrate the energy. And yet the crystal still didn't budge.

Prue couldn't resist. Carefully controlling her own power, she moved the amethyst a few centimeters.

Adrienne broke into a grin. "I can't believe it," she said. "I found it. I found the power."

"You sure did," Prue said. "Listen, I've got to run now. I'll see you later, okay?"

"Oh, I'm sure that you will," Adrienne said.

Prue left the shop grinning. For once she felt positively cheerful about being a witch. It was fun to help a friend.

Prue hummed to herself as she unwrapped the pretty bottle she'd bought at Full Moon. She set it on the edge of the mantel in the parlor and stepped back to admire the effect. Perfect. The blue of the bottle completely fit with the room's decor.

Just as I feel Adrienne and I fit together, Prue thought. It was so good to connect with someone other than her sisters. It had been so long since she had even tried. Thank goodness Adrienne hadn't disappointed her.

She crumpled up the paper bag from Full

Moon, and noticed something fall to the floor. Prue stooped to pick it up. A tiny red satin ribbon with a knot in the middle. Must be a scrap from one of Adrienne's gift-wrapping jobs, she figured. She placed it back inside the bag.

"Prue!" Piper's voice called from the front hall.

"I'm in here!" Prue shouted a response.

She heard her sister's footsteps approaching. The parlor door slammed open. "Hey, I—"

Prue sucked in a breath. The blue bottle teetered. It was about to fall off the mantel! She centered her energy and sent a small blast of it at the bottle, to right it.

Crash. The bottle hit the hardwood floor and shattered on impact. Piper let out a small squeak of surprise. "Did I do that?" she asked. "Oh my gosh, I'm so sorry."

Prue frowned. That was weird. Why hadn't she been able to push the bottle? Maybe she'd been distracted by Piper's entrance into the room.

"Prue?" Piper said. "Really. I'm so sorry. I'll buy you a new—whatever that was."

"No, no, it's okay. I shouldn't have put it so close to the edge." Prue walked to the kitchen to grab a broom and dustpan. She tried to dismiss the incident, but no matter how hard she tried, she couldn't help feeling unnerved. Her powers had never just totally blanked out on her before. What had happened this time to make things different?

CHAPTER
10

Phoebe folded her umbrella shut and stepped into the entry of Toscana. She blinked in surprise. From the outside, the restaurant looked like another brick building in the Embarcadero. Inside, the walls were the color of old parchment, the floor a deep red tile. A fire danced in a stone hearth, and hand-painted Italian plates hung on the walls.

"*Buona sera, Signorina,*" the maitre d' greeted her. "How many are in your party?"

"Two," Phoebe answered. "I'm here to meet Kenji Yamada."

"Right this way." The maitre d' led her through a stone archway to a smaller back room whose French doors looked out onto a rainy courtyard filled with green, leafy plants and colorful flowers.

Kenji stood up as she approached the table. "I was hoping we'd get a table in the courtyard, but this weather . . ."

"This is great," Phoebe assured him. "I feel like I'm in the kitchen of a beautiful old Italian country house."

"That's exactly how you're supposed to feel," their waiter confirmed. He set menus, fresh bread, and a small cruet of olive oil on the table.

"You look beautiful," Kenji said when the waiter had left.

Phoebe smiled. "You mean my semi-medieval look?"

She had tried on six different outfits before settling on this one, a long-sleeved burgundy velvet dress from a vintage shop. Normally, Phoebe liked her dresses short and close-fitting. This one was different. It had a low-cut square neck, and a luxurious calf-length skirt that draped from the high waist. Judging from Kenji's gaze, she'd made the right choice.

"I think you look lovely," Kenji said. He handed Phoebe a long-stemmed red rose. It had a small matching satin ribbon knotted around the stem.

"Oh, this is so pretty!" Phoebe took the rose. "Thank you." Her eyes met his and a shiver of pleasure went through her. He seemed to have been looking forward to this date as much as she had.

She ran her finger lightly along his strong jaw. "The bruise on your face is almost gone," she observed.

He smiled. "I can barely feel it now."

"So you're glad you went through with the tournament?"

"Because of how well I placed, Sensei Towers gave me permission to take some of his more advanced classes." He shrugged. "Besides, I've found it's good to confront the things that scare you."

Sometimes it seemed to Phoebe that ever since she and her sisters had discovered their powers, that's all they'd done. "I don't know," she disagreed. "I think I'd be very happy without some of those confrontations."

One of Kenji's dark eyebrows rose. "What do you mean? Do you make a habit of walking into scary situations?"

"Well, I'm taking karate," she improvised quickly. "So far it's been fine. But the fighting part scares me a little."

"I'm not crazy about that aspect myself," Kenji confessed. "Some people are drawn to martial arts because they're aggressive."

Phoebe nodded. The same way some people are drawn to the dark arts, she thought.

"I like it for the way my body feels when I'm training," Kenji explained.

And I like the way it looks, Phoebe added silently. Kenji was wearing an off-white collarless shirt and khakis. His sleeves were rolled up to reveal tanned, muscled forearms. Phoebe sighed happily. She loved well-built arms.

The waiter reappeared at their table. Phoebe

ordered grilled polenta with portobello mushrooms. Kenji ordered pasta with an asparagus
cream sauce.

"So, tell me about you," Kenji said a moment
later. "I want to know absolutely everything. So
far, all I've got is that you used to live in New
York, you've moved back home, and"—he leaned
across the table—"you're a phenomenal kisser."

"Well . . . I'm in between things right now,"
Phoebe began. "I mean, I haven't quite figured
out what I want to do with my life. My sisters are
both totally driven—Prue is an art specialist at an
auction house, and Piper just opened a totally hot
nightclub—but I'm still trying to figure out what
I want to be when I grow up."

Kenji ran a gentle finger along the back of her
hand. "You sound as if you think there's something wrong with that."

"Well, let's just say my older sister Prue would
be very relieved if I got a steady job."

Kenji snapped his fingers. "I know just the
thing! Have you ever considered engineering?"

Phoebe laughed. "That's too radical. Prue might
actually have to approve of me if I did that."

"She's really hard on you," Kenji observed.

Phoebe tilted her head and rested her chin in
her palm. Kenji was so easy to talk to. She thought
a moment about her relationship with Prue. "No.
It's just that Prue and I are so different. It makes
living under the same roof a little . . . tense. But we
really love each other," she added hastily.

Kenji smiled at her. "I can't wait to meet them."

"Are you sure you're ready for that?" Phoebe asked, only half joking.

"Phoebe, I want to get to know you. That means getting to know your family, too. Besides, I have a feeling that seeing the three Halliwell sisters together could be pretty interesting."

Their dinners arrived, and for a while neither of them said much except to comment on how delicious the food was. When the waiter offered them dessert menus, Phoebe groaned. "I can't eat another bite."

"Me either," Kenji agreed. He signaled for the check.

Phoebe felt a stab of disappointment. *Is the date over already? Maybe I should have ordered the chocolate soufflé—it takes ages to prepare.*

"I have an idea." Kenji nodded toward the French doors. "It looks like the rain has stopped. How about a walk?"

Phoebe and Kenji strolled along the Embarcadero—the bayside promenade that lined the eastern waterfront of the city. The air was chilly but the clouds had cleared, and the lights along the shoreline glittered gold against the night.

"Phoebe," Kenji stopped walking. He took her hand and drew her close. "There's something I've been wanting to say to you all night."

Phoebe's pulse began to race. "What is it?"

"I just want you to know . . ." He paused, as if searching for the right words. "I think that you're sweet and smart and funny and so beautiful it's driving me crazy."

Phoebe looked deeply into Kenji's eyes. She searched for any sign of a lie, of deception. Could this wonderful, gorgeous guy really mean all the things he was saying to her?

"You don't believe me." Kenji's voice was soft.

"I'm—I'm afraid to," Phoebe confessed. How could she tell him that ever since discovering her powers, she'd lived with the nagging fear that evil was everywhere?

Kenji wrapped his arms around her. "Maybe it's time I eased some of your doubts," he murmured, his voice husky.

Phoebe inhaled the crisp, woodsy scent of his cologne. For a long moment they just held each other, like friends who'd found each other after having been separated for a lifetime. Then his hand caressed the side of her face and lifted it to his. Phoebe felt a thrill go through her as their lips met. Everything about being this close to Kenji felt right—his touch, his scent, his taste. The kiss was warm and passionate, as if neither one of them could bear for it to end.

Phoebe was the one who broke away, shaken by the intensity. How was she supposed to take it slow when she felt like this? When she wanted him so much?

Kenji gently brushed back a strand of her hair. "And you don't believe I really like you?" he asked.

Phoebe turned her face so his hand cupped her cheek. "Okay. I believe you."

"Why don't we go home," he suggested.

"You mean to your place?"

He nodded. "We'd have all ten square feet of it to ourselves."

Phoebe laughed. "Sounds enticing." She shut her eyes. "But I can't."

"What do you mean? Phoebe, look at me. What's wrong?"

Phoebe opened her eyes and met his questioning look. She saw his confusion and hated that she was causing it. "Nothing's wrong," she explained. "And that's why I can't."

Kenji's eyebrows raised. "You lost me there."

"Kenji, I can't, because everything about being with you feels right. I don't want to rush into things and blow it."

She saw understanding come into his eyes. "That's what you're afraid of?" he asked gently.

Phoebe nodded.

"Can you *see* that happening—in the future?"

Phoebe stopped short. Her breath caught in her throat. What did Kenji mean? Did he have some clue about her power? She searched his eyes again. His gaze was warm and loving. No, she decided. It couldn't be.

"I'm not running away from you," she assured him. "I just need to take this slowly."

"Okay." He drew her back into his arms. "But don't think you're getting away from me so easily." He fingered the ribbon tied around her rose. "Sooner or later, Phoebe, you will be completely under my spell."

*   *   *

A sweet, heavy smell rose from the cauldron on the hearth. The Master lit the two three-armed candelabras, then took his place before the altar.

He began the Latin incantations, and his followers joined in.

The large crystal that was suspended above them began to glow, and though the windows were boarded up and the door shut, a wind swept through the room. The flames on the candles danced wildly, creating monstrous shadows along the walls.

The Master spoke. "We have been making progress in our battle against the Charmed Ones, and I am pleased," he announced. "We have discovered that the middle sister can freeze time. It was this power that she used to ensnare our brother warlock."

A murmur of acknowledgment sounded from some of the coven members. "Now, as to the other sisters—what have my spiders uncovered?"

Slowly two figures in black robes stepped forward. They knelt before him.

"Kenji?" the Master said.

The young man got to his feet. "I believe that the youngest sister, Phoebe, has the power to predict the future. But I don't think she has much control over what it is she sees."

The Master turned to Adrienne. "And you?"

Adrienne stood. "The oldest sister, Prue, has the power of telekinesis. She demonstrated it in my shop."

"Excellent. You've done well." The Master waved his two "spiders" back into the crowd.

"Together these witches are formidable, but not invincible," the Master assured his coven. "We have the crystal. We have the combined power of every warlock in this room. And we have the red talisman. My brothers and sisters, these witches will be destroyed!"

"Wait!" Adrienne spoke up.

"What is it?" the Master inquired.

"Isn't there another way to deal with the Charmed Ones?" she asked.

"What other way?" he barked, his words harsh.

Adrienne blanched but persisted. "Can't the coven just take their powers? Why must they be killed?"

"Because, my innocent little spider," the Master said, his tone dripping with venom, "if they are vessels for power now, what is to stop them from becoming filled with it again?"

The Master raised his arms. "The Charmed Ones are to be destroyed!" he shouted. "Destroyed!" The coven took up the chant, its cadence whirling through the dark room.

CHAPTER
11

The next day at dusk, Prue strolled along Twenty-fourth Street, lightly swinging a small shopping bag. Many of the shops she passed were closing, but the street was busy with people rushing home from work, stopping to pick up food for dinner, or already forming lines for the Noe Valley's trendier restaurants.

Prue scooted around the tables of a sidewalk café and the delicious aroma of espresso stopped her. She'd had a long day at Buckland's. Maybe she should go in and recaffeinate?

Not tonight, she decided. She'd be cutting it too close if she stopped. She wanted to get home to wrap the present she'd bought Phoebe before her sister got home from karate class.

She switched her bag to the other hand, pleased with her purchase. She'd bought a packet of *Herba euphrasia*, and a beautiful handmade blue ceramic jar to keep it in. She'd noticed the herb when she'd been in Full Moon the day before, and she'd looked it up in *The Book of Shadows* that night.

"When steeped in a tea it doth soothe one's sleep and enhance visions of future days," the book had read. It seemed tailor-made as a peace offering for Phoebe.

Not that she and Phoebe had been fighting lately, but there always seemed to be a thin line of tension between them. It was a line that Prue wanted badly to dissolve.

Prue sighed. She knew Phoebe thought that she didn't approve of her. Admittedly, Prue wasn't wild about Phoebe's work ethic. But since they'd come into their powers, she'd gained new respect for her youngest sister. Phoebe was the first one to take *The Book of Shadows* seriously. Since then, she seemed to have a special bond with the book. And it was Phoebe who had convinced Prue and Piper of the truth—that they were witches. Beyond her gift to see into the future, Phoebe had an intuitiveness that Prue was learning to trust.

And Piper . . . Prue had been so difficult while Piper was trying to do something kindhearted at the Sunrise Center. Celeste and Daria seemed like good kids, even if Daria did get a little riled up at the house. She'd have to make up her behavior to Piper and her mentorees, too, she realized. She promised herself that she'd do it soon.

Prue hurried toward her car, wanting to beat the rush hour traffic. She hoped her sister would like the gift. If I've got the right herb, that is, she thought. She opened the bag to check. No, Adrienne had given her the right ingredient this time.

Of course she had! Prue admonished herself. Stop being so mistrustful. Adrienne is your friend, remember? Then Prue noticed something else in the bag.

That's weird. She lifted another bright red ribbon, knotted at the center, from the bag. It was the second time she'd found one of these. How did it get in there?

She crossed the street, staring at the ribbon. A car horn blared, and her head jerked up. She hadn't been paying attention! A huge SUV was barreling toward her. In a flash Prue sent out a blast of power to stop the SUV. I hope it doesn't hit the car behind it, she thought.

But the SUV didn't stop at all. Prue froze as it sped directly toward her!

A loud, hysterical scream sounded from Prue's throat. A strong arm wrapped around her waist and jerked her out of the street.

Prue and her rescuer fell to the sidewalk. She looked up. A gangly teenage boy scrambled to his knees beside her. "Are you okay?" he asked.

"I—I think so," Prue stammered.

"That SUV almost mowed you down," the kid told her. "You walked out right in front of it. Why didn't you move out of the way?"

"I—I guess I was distracted," Prue said. She sat up, knowing she was still shaking too much to attempt standing. Her arm had been scraped in the fall, but that was her only injury. She checked the bag. The blue ceramic jar was still in one piece.

But inside her, she felt as though something had been shattered. She was safe now, and yet she was more frightened than she'd ever been. Her power had never failed her so miserably before.

Her rescuer got to his feet and held out his hand to help her up. Prue took it gratefully. "Thank you," she said. "You saved my life."

The boy's face turned bright red. "No big deal," he told her. "Just be careful, okay?"

"I will," Prue promised.

Despite her original plans, she went into the café and bought herself a cup of hot chamomile tea. She didn't trust herself to get into her car and drive.

What just happened? she asked herself. Why couldn't I push that car? She took a deep breath and tried to calm her mind. She had to look at this logically. I *know* I used my power, she reasoned. But the car came straight at me. Almost as if my power was reversed.

That can't be, she thought. And yet she had a scraped arm that proved that it could. She felt fear surging back into her. Her hand trembled so badly that she had to put down the mug of hot tea before she spilled it.

I don't understand, she thought. How could my powers just backfire?

Phoebe was tired and sweaty when Sensei Towers ended class that evening, and her rib cage was sore from a kick she'd taken during sparring. The last one to leave the floor, she slumped toward the women's locker room, rubbing her side.

"Hey. You on the injured list?"

She glanced up to see Kenji standing in the doorway of the men's locker room. Phoebe guessed that he was there to take the more advanced class that followed hers. She hadn't seen him since two nights before, when she'd opted not to go home with him. She wondered if he'd really been okay with her decision.

"I think I'll live," she told him, deciding to play it light. "I'm just a little sore."

"I saw the kick that nailed you," Kenji said. "If you want, we can work out together later this week. I'll show you how you can counter an attack like that."

"Sounds like a good idea," Phoebe told him. "I'm kind of fond of my ribs. I'd like them to stay intact."

"I'm fond of your ribs, too," Kenji said, flashing a sexy smile. Phoebe instantly relaxed. Everything was fine.

"You know, I've got a homeopathic cream in my locker that really helps with bruises," he continued. "If you wait here a second, I'll get it for you."

"Sure." Phoebe watched him disappear into the men's locker room. He is just too cool, she decided, and so totally sweet.

Moments later Kenji handed her a tube of cream. "Rub it on a few times a day. It'll ease the pain and heal the bruise a lot faster."

"Yes, doctor," she teased.

"And be sure to call me in the morning," he added.

Was he being serious? Did he want her to call him? "Uh . . . I would, Doc, but I don't have the number for your office."

"Hmm," Kenji said. "I'd give it to you, only . . . my class is going to start in five minutes, and I've got to stretch out and practice a kata. How about we just make a date for tomorrow night?"

Phoebe gave him a mock frown. "I'll have to have my secretary check my book," she said in a formal voice, then grinned. "But I don't think that I'll have any conflicts."

"Great, I'll meet you here at seven, and then we'll figure out what we want to do." Kenji leaned forward, brushed her lips with a quick kiss, then went to stretch.

Phoebe floated toward the locker room in a happy daze. She glanced at herself in the mirror. Her gi was soaked with sweat, her hair was plastered to her forehead. Yuck! She was a complete mess, and Kenji had *still* asked her out. He was almost too good to be true!

Phoebe giggled as she took off her gi and rubbed the cream into her tender side. She finished dressing, stuffed her soggy gi into her pack, and brushed her hair. Then she put on her favorite thick, hooded sweatshirt and zipped it up. She was still sweaty and didn't want to risk getting a chill once she got outside.

When she emerged from the women's locker room, Kenji was alone on the floor, practicing his kata. She watched for a moment as he executed a perfect spinning back kick, then moved smoothly into a series of strikes. He was concentrating so hard that he didn't even notice her standing there.

Oh well, she thought. So I don't have his undivided attention. He's still pretty wonderful.

Phoebe bowed as she left the dojo, then jogged to the end of the block where she'd left her car. She yanked open the door—the lock was broken, and she hadn't had time to get it repaired—then slid into the driver's seat. She dropped her pack beside her. She was about to pull out her keys when she noticed something sticking out beneath the pack. She tugged on it.

A red ribbon with a knot in the center. That's odd, she thought. How had it gotten into her car? Maybe it had fallen off the rose Kenji had given her and stuck to the bottom of her pack when she'd left the house? Who knew?

With a shrug Phoebe fumbled in her purse for her keys. Her fingers wrapped around Kenji's homeopathic cream. She jerked in her seat as light flashed into her eyes. She was about to have a premonition. Its images floated in front of her:

She and Kenji alone in the dojo, both dressed in their white gis. She kissed him, just as she had ten minutes ago. Then she saw herself dressed as she was now, leaving the dojo.

Kenji practicing—powerful movements, intense concentration. So intense that he doesn't realize there was someone else in the room with him—a tall man in a black robe—with a gleaming knife, plunging down toward Kenji!

The vision ended.

"No!" Phoebe screamed. She bolted out of the car and back toward the dojo. Her injured rib burned, but she pushed the pain aside. She had to get to Kenji.

She threw open the door to the dojo, her heart pounding. "Kenji?" she called. But the room was empty.

She stepped onto the wooden floor. The dojo was eerily quiet. Where was everyone? she wondered. Wasn't there supposed to be an advanced class starting soon? And where was Kenji?

She caught a movement in the mirror. She spun around and gasped. The black-robed attacker from her vision raced toward her. She couldn't see his face beneath the hood, but the glinting silver knife was frighteningly clear.

Terror pushed all her karate moves from her mind. She charged for the door. "Aagh!" she screamed. She felt a sharp tug on the hood of her sweatshirt. Her hands flew to her throat—the neckline was choking her. Her attacker used the hood to drag her toward him. Phoebe's knees buckled, and she sank to the floor.

The man in the black robe released her hood. Phoebe coughed and sputtered, gasping for air. She glanced up to see the man raise the blade. But before he could plunge the knife into her, a deafening cry startled them both. The man's head whipped around, giving Phoebe the chance to crawl away.

Sensei Towers launched himself at the hooded man. He grabbed the arm that held the knife and thrust a powerful front kick at the man's elbow. Phoebe heard a sickening snap as her attacker's arm broke in two. The man in the black robe dropped the knife with a scream of anguish.

"Phoebe!" Sensei Towers knelt beside her. The attacker fled out the front door. Sensei Towers moved to stop the man—but it was too late.

"Are you okay? Did he cut you?" Phoebe's teacher asked.

"No," she answered. "You stopped him before he could."

The karate teacher quickly took her pulse. He rocked back on his heels. "You seem to be fine," he told her. "Will you be okay if I leave you for a minute to call nine-one-one?"

Phoebe nodded and sat up. She leaned heavily against the nearest wall. She'd almost been killed by some lunatic with a knife. If she had to guess, she'd guess a warlock.

She shuddered, realizing that the trouble-free

lull was over. But what really spooked her was that, for the first time ever, her vision was totally off the mark. What she saw *wasn't* what had actually happened.

Somehow, something was terribly wrong with her power.

CHAPTER

12

Piper was in the club's storeroom, doing her weekly Monday afternoon inventory. She checked the metal shelves of supplies, muttering to herself. "Order more paper towels, we're fine on napkins, running low on coasters for the bar . . ."

She heard a knock on the open storeroom door, and glanced up from her clipboard. Celeste was standing there, dark shadows beneath her pale blue eyes.

"Celeste, are you okay?" Piper asked.

"I'm surviving," the girl replied.

It had been only a couple of days since they'd escaped from the house on Colwood Street. Had something new happened? Had Celeste been pursued by another warlock?

Piper put down the clipboard. "How about I get us a couple of sodas?"

"Sure," Celeste said.

Piper got the sodas and joined Celeste at a table.

"You look like you didn't get much sleep last night," Piper observed.

"I didn't," Celeste admitted. "I kept thinking about the house." She gave Piper a wary look.

Piper's throat tightened. Did Celeste remember her casting spells? Or anything about the time-freeze? Did Celeste know she was a witch?

"What about the house?" she prompted.

"I remember going in on my own and walking up that staircase. I remember someone in a hooded robe and a horrible green light. And I remember screaming for you." Celeste shuddered. "Then there's this big blank in my memory. All I remember after that is the two of us getting out of that place."

Piper felt her dread dissolve. "But what's happened since then? Are you okay?" she asked.

Celeste nodded. "But I'm worried. Daria came back last night. She was totally weird. It's almost like she's . . . possessed."

Piper felt a flash of alarm. Maybe that's what was going on with Daria. Maybe an evil spirit had gotten hold of her. She and her sisters had certainly seen cases like that before.

Celeste pushed her soda away. "That's why I'm here. Daria was so mad at you the other day. I was afraid she might hurt you. I mean, yesterday she told me if I slept in our room, she'd kill me. She even showed me a knife."

"She *what?*" Piper gasped. "Where did you sleep last night?"

"On one of the picnic benches in the dining room," Celeste answered. "It's the only common room that's left open at night."

"Did you tell Mr. Morgan about this?"

Celeste rolled her eyes. "Daria would only deny it if I did."

"Do you want me to talk to Mr. Morgan to see if he'll give you a different room?" Piper asked.

"The center's full," Celeste replied flatly. "He can't transfer me to another room without putting someone else in with Daria. And I'm not so sure that's a good idea."

"Me either," Piper admitted with a sigh.

She thought about her options for all of three minutes before realizing there was really only one. "Celeste," she said, "would you like to stay at our house for a while?"

A wary look came back into Celeste's eyes. "You don't really mean that."

"I wouldn't have said it if I didn't."

"But your sisters—"

"My sisters will understand," Piper said with more certainty than she felt.

Celeste didn't meet her eyes. She traced invisible patterns on the surface of the table with her finger. She's afraid, Piper realized. She's afraid to say yes—to take a chance on us and be disappointed.

"Celeste, you can't stay at the center if you're in danger from Daria."

Celeste raised her head. "I'd feel funny just showing up at your house."

"What if I talk to my sisters and they say they *want* you to move in?"

Celeste flashed her a wry smile. "Yeah, and you've got a bridge to Oakland that you want to sell me, right?"

Piper ignored the sarcasm. "I'll call home now," she said. She punched in the number. After three rings, she hung up. "Nobody home," she reported.

Celeste stood. "I'll be okay at the center. Really, the dining hall isn't so bad."

Piper knew she really had to warn her sisters before she had Celeste move in. "Listen to me. Tomorrow, after I talk with my sisters, I'm going to come pick you up. You're staying with us."

Celeste threw her arms around Piper. "I hope so," she whimpered.

Piper returned to the stockroom troubled. She couldn't let Celeste down. She had to come up with a plan. The least she could do, she decided, was to call Mr. Morgan and tell him what was going on with Daria. He'd have to find Celeste a safe place to stay then—at least for tonight. Then she could get his permission to have Celeste come to her house for a while.

She reached for her purse. She had his card in there somewhere. Was it in her wallet? No. Her date book? No. She pulled out three other business cards, none of them for the Sunrise Center. She felt something in the bottom of her purse that she didn't recognize.

Piper's eyebrows rose in surprise as she lifted

out a red ribbon, knotted in the middle. Where did this come from? she wondered. She tossed it into the trash.

She was just reaching for the phone to call information when she heard a vibrating sound behind her. She turned to see a tall metal shelving unit, loaded with heavy canned goods, teetering.

She watched in shock as it began to fall toward her. Piper threw up her hands—a reaction that usually froze time.

But the shelving continued to fall. For the space of a heartbeat, Piper felt stuck in place, unable to move out of the way, unable to summon the power that would save her.

She screamed as the shelf swayed forward and the heavy cans tumbled through the air.

"Piper!" Joey, the busboy, lunged at her, shoving her out of the way. He spun and grabbed the shelving unit and steadied it. Slowly he pushed it back against the wall. "This thing is not stable. We'd better clear off these shelves."

"That's a plan," Piper agreed, hoping her voice didn't betray how frightened she was.

Joey kept up a stream of chatter, but Piper barely heard him. Her mind kept replaying that moment when time should have frozen, but it didn't.

She tried it again, focusing, aiming her powers. Still, nothing happened. Joey continued talking, and for a split second, Piper felt stuck in place.

What's happening to me? she asked herself. What's going on with my powers?

CHAPTER
13

On Tuesday morning Prue called in sick. She felt a twinge of guilt as she lied to her assistant at Buckland's, but she figured the loss of her powers qualified as some sort of health risk. Mostly, though, she'd stayed home because the problem warranted a family meeting.

Prue set a tray containing three mugs of coffee on the end table in the living room. She took the black coffee for herself, then waited impatiently for her sisters to join her.

Phoebe emerged from the kitchen seconds later, carrying a bowl of granola and a chocolate donut. Piper trailed her, bringing in a fruit salad, spoons, and three bowls.

Piper glanced down at Phoebe's plate. "Don't the granola and the donut kind of cancel each other out?"

"Possibly." Phoebe arranged herself comfortably on the couch. She reached for a coffee mug, sniffed it, then frowned at its contents. "Yuck. How can you ruin perfectly good coffee with soy milk?" she asked, handing the mug to Piper.

"I put half and half in yours," Prue assured Phoebe. "Now enough about breakfast. There's something I need to talk to you about."

"Uh—I've got a little subject I want to discuss, too," Piper said in a grim tone.

Phoebe winced. "Why do I have the feeling that the agenda for this meeting is 'trouble.' With a capital 'Big'?"

"Because it is," Prue told her. "Something happened to me yesterday. I wasn't paying attention when I crossed the street, and I suddenly realized an SUV was coming straight at me. When I tried to use my power to push it back, it swerved *toward* me. It nearly ran me down."

"Oh my gosh," Piper declared. "My powers didn't work yesterday either. Instead of freezing time, I think—I think I froze myself. I nearly got brained by a shelfful of heavy, falling canned goods."

Phoebe looked stunned. "I thought it was just me," she said. "And that it was a freak thing."

Prue felt her stomach churning. "Let me guess," she said. "You had a vision and it didn't come true?"

"Not exactly," Phoebe explained. "I had a vision last night. I saw Kenji being attacked in the dojo."

"Who's Kenji?" Prue asked.

Piper and Phoebe exchanged a quick glance.

"A guy. A guy I like. So, anyway," Phoebe went on, "I ran back into the dojo and Kenji wasn't being attacked at all. He wasn't even there. But the next thing I knew, *I* was being attacked by the guy in my vision."

"What happened?" Prue asked, alarmed. "Are you all right?"

"Sensei Towers came to my rescue. But it could have been really nasty."

Piper shut her eyes. "There are definitely warlocks involved here."

"Well, at least one of them has a broken arm," Phoebe said with satisfaction.

"Wait—there's a pattern," Prue said. "Not only are our powers not working, they seem to be inverted—doing the exact opposite of what they're supposed to do. We've barely had a chance to be in the same room in the last three days, and yet the same something or someone seems to be attacking each one of us."

"As in, someone's put a spell on us?" Phoebe picked at her fruit salad.

"Maybe it was that night you two came to the club," Piper suggested. "Remember, I saw someone at the window."

Prue shook her head. "We still don't know for sure that anyone was there," she pointed out. "Besides, that was a week ago. These—malfunctions—just started recently. I think someone got to us in the last couple of days."

"I think I know how this all started. I had a bit of a warlock encounter," Piper admitted.

Prue listened with a combination of concern and outrage as Piper told her about the house on Colwood Street. "When did this happen?" she asked, her voice sharper than she meant it to be.

"On Friday," Piper answered.

"And when were you planning on telling us about it?" Prue demanded. "Piper, you know we have to stick together."

Piper met her gaze. "I know that," she said. "I didn't mention it because I knew you'd lecture me all over again about mentoring. But Celeste needs my help, now more than ever."

"And how are you going to help her if you can't even use your powers?" Prue asked softly.

"I don't know." Piper slumped back against the couch. "But from what I can tell, Daria's seriously mixed up in black magic. And she's made threats against Celeste. I want Celeste to stay with us for a while."

"You want *what?*" Prue snapped. "Piper, have you lost it? I cannot believe what a phenomenally bad idea that is."

"Prue's right," Phoebe said. "We're all under attack, we can't trust our powers to work properly, and you want some innocent kid we can't even protect to stay with us?"

"Look, I don't know what else to do," Piper admitted.

Prue was getting more worried by the second. She stood and paced the living room. "Okay," she said, trying to calm herself. "Let's hold off on making a decision about Celeste. First we've got to find a way to control this situation before it controls us."

"Good idea," Phoebe agreed.

"Let's figure out who's attacking, and what we're going to do about it," Prue continued. She couldn't help glaring at Piper. "If Daria's mixed up in black magic, then she could be the one behind this."

"Could she have cast a spell, or planted something in the house the day that she was here?" Phoebe asked.

"I suppose," Piper reluctantly agreed. "But what could she plant?"

Prue remembered the phone call she overheard at the Full Moon. The customer Adrienne refused to "aid and abet" in their black magic. The customer wanted steel nails and— "How about dolls? Have either of you found anything like that?"

Piper groaned. "I found one in Daria's drawer in the center," Piper confessed. She thought for a moment. "But we haven't found anything like that here."

"Wait a minute!" Phoebe sat upright, looking excited. "Yesterday, right before my not-vision, I noticed something in my car. A red ribbon knotted in the middle. I thought it might have been from Kenji's rose, but when I got home, I saw that it wasn't."

Prue felt a chill go through her. She stopped

pacing. "I found a red ribbon, too," she said. "Right before I almost got flattened by the urban attack vehicle. Only, mine was in a bag of things I bought at Full Moon."

Piper sighed. "Mine was in my purse. I found it a few minutes before the canned-food avalanche."

Prue tried to piece the information together. It did not compute. Daria couldn't have put something in the bag from the Wicca shop. And how would she even know what Phoebe's car looked like? Someone else had to be involved.

Piper ran her fingers through her long, dark hair. "Maybe Daria has something to do with it," she allowed. "But that house was drenched with black magic. I can't help feeling we're up against something much bigger than a resentful thirteen-year-old."

"Agreed," Prue said. "So why don't we start with our one known factor?"

"We have one?" Phoebe inquired.

"The evil red ribbons," Prue said. "Do either of you still have yours?"

Piper shuddered. "I threw mine out the minute I found it."

"I looked for it when I went back to my car," Phoebe said. "It was gone."

"Mine's gone, too," Prue said. "I think I dropped it when my rescuer tackled me." She paused. "I think we're overdue for a consultation with *The Book of Shadows*. Maybe there's something in there about red ribbons or inverted powers."

"I'll get it," Phoebe volunteered. She headed for the attic.

Prue turned to Piper. Her face looked ashen. It's Piper's good heart that got her into this mess, she reminded herself. I should go a little easier on her. "Are you okay?" she asked.

Piper bit her lip. "I'm sorry," she said, her voice quivered. "You and Phoebe were right. It was crazy of me to think I could be a mentor. But now we're in this mess, and I can't abandon Celeste."

"I know." Prue sat down on the couch beside Piper and hugged her. "I know."

Phoebe dashed back down the stairs, carrying *The Book of Shadows*. She laid it on the table, frowning as she flipped through it. "I see spells involving buttons, strands of hair, crystals, gloves, sealing wax . . . but nothing with ribbons." She glanced up at her sisters. "Don't you wish this thing had an index?"

"Or a table of contents," Piper agreed wistfully. "Even chapter titles would be nice."

"Want me to try?" Prue offered. She was not the type given to fanciful thoughts, but for a while now she'd been thinking of the book as— not exactly a creature—but something alive— with a will and power of its own. It sometimes cooperated and opened exactly to the page you needed. Other times you could spend hours deciphering a hand-scrawled spell, only to realize that it was not what you needed at all. The book, Prue knew, was in its own way teaching them.

And for each of the three Halliwell sisters it provided different lessons.

"Knock yourself out," Phoebe said, handing her the heavy leather-bound volume.

Prue sat down with the open book on her lap. She closed her eyes and envisioned the ribbon. It was about two inches long and half an inch wide, made of bright red satin. The knot in its center had been tied deliberately, neatly.

She opened her eyes, silently asking the book to help them. A breeze filtered through the room, and the book's pages began to stir. The breeze intensified, and the pages turned faster and faster.

Prue held her breath as the breeze vanished as suddenly as it had risen. The book lay open to a page that showed a tall, robed figure, an athame bound to his waist.

"The Coven of the New Sun," she read aloud.

Phoebe lifted an eyebrow in surprise. "That doesn't even sound remotely dark. Could they be a *good* coven?"

Prue read on for a bit. "No. Apparently the 'new sun' refers to a source of power that they call on. This doesn't say what that power source is, but they are *so* not the good guys." Prue checked the date on the page. "Back in eighteen eighty-eight they were trying to destroy our ancestors. I don't think a lot has changed since then."

"Is there anything about the red ribbons?" Piper asked.

"Here," Prue said, pointing to a tiny illustration on the bottom of the page. "The ribbons are magic talismans of some kind. They're used as both the coven's calling cards and to activate spells that the coven has put in place."

"Calling cards," Piper echoed. "Well, at least they've got manners."

Prue squinted, thinking. "Calling cards were in vogue near the turn of the century. It was a very Victorian thing to do, an expected social grace among the upper classes. You had your servant deliver your card to someone before you called on them."

"So that means we can expect visitors?" Phoebe asked tensely.

"That's as good a guess as any," Prue agreed. "We've got to cast a protection spell, pronto!"

Piper's voice was bleak. "It may not work with our powers all screwed up. What if it backfires like the spells we cast yesterday?"

"We've got to try," Prue decided. She searched through the book for a protection spell she'd seen earlier. "Here it is," she said. "We'll need sage, salt, a shell for burning the sage, poke root, yarrow, a white candle, and some ingredients I bought at Full Moon," she said. "I'll go get those."

"I'm on the white candle and shell," Phoebe said. "And matches, of course."

"That leaves me with sage, salt, yarrow, and poke root," Piper said, starting for the kitchen.

Five minutes later they'd collected the ingredients for the spell. Phoebe placed some of the dried sage in the shell, lit it, then blew out the flame so that the sage began to smoke. As its scent filled the house, Piper lit the white candle.

Prue held a pinch of salt between her fingers and closed her eyes, concentrating on purifying the energy in the house.

She opened her eyes. They were ready to begin. She passed her hand through the sage's smoke, then picked up the poke root.

" 'Power from sky above, power from earth below . . .' *Who is that?*" she asked, totally losing track of the spell. A handsome young man stood peering in the living room window.

Her sisters whirled around to look. "Oh, my God," Phoebe murmured. "It's Kenji!"

Kenji held up a hand, his face set in a grim expression.

"Is he waving at me?" Phoebe wondered aloud.

"I knew we should have done the spell in the attic!" Piper muttered. "I should have said something."

"Too late now," Prue said. "Phoebe, go talk to him and convince him we were—I don't know—rehearsing for a community play or something."

"Right!" Phoebe ran for the door.

Prue exchanged a glance with Piper. "That didn't go well."

"It didn't go at all," Piper agreed.

The phone rang then. "Let the machine get it," Prue said. "When Phoebe comes back, we'll try the spell again—in the attic."

Piper gathered up the ingredients. She stopped as she heard the panicked voice on the answering machine.

"Piper, it's me. Daria's gone over the top. Way over. Last night, when I slept in the dining hall, she slashed the sheets on my bed to shreds. Please! You have to help me!"

CHAPTER
14

Piper raced for the phone and snatched it up. "Hello? Hello?" She gave a growl of frustration and hung up. "Too late," she muttered. She turned to Prue.

Prue sighed. "You want to go get her now, don't you?"

"I've got to," Piper said.

"I know you want to protect Celeste," Prue said carefully. "But maybe it would make more sense to just remove the threat."

"What do you mean?" Piper asked, confused.

"I mean, can't the people who run the Sunrise Center do something about Daria?"

"You would think so," Piper replied. "I called Mr. Morgan, the director, yesterday and told him what was going on with Daria. He said he'd keep an eye on her, but he's obviously not doing anything about it. Celeste shouldn't have to spend her nights bedding down in the dining hall."

"No, of course not." Prue rubbed her forehead. Piper could tell she was debating the situation. She didn't want Celeste to be in danger, but she didn't want her around the house either. "What if we got Celeste a hotel room for a few nights?" she suggested.

"In this city?" Piper asked. "Have you suddenly come into a trust fund you didn't tell me about?"

"Then we'll find a cheap motel," Prue told her.

"No, Prue! No way!" Piper shrieked.

Prue's eyes widened at Piper's outburst. Good, Piper thought. Maybe she'll realize how serious I am about this.

"Celeste is alone and she's scared," she said, her voice shaking with fury. "The last thing I'm going to do is put her somewhere she'll be even *more* alone and scared. And I couldn't live with myself if she stayed at the center and Daria hurt her."

Piper took a breath to calm herself down a little. "I don't have another option. I've got to get her out of there, and I've got to keep her safe. This is the only place I can bring her."

"You realize that our house may be just as dangerous for Celeste. Or worse. At least until we've dealt with this coven." Prue tried one last warning.

"I know," Piper said. "But here at least we can try to protect her."

"We can *try*," Prue agreed unhappily.

Piper gave her a quick hug. "I'm out of here," she declared. "I'll be back with Celeste as fast as I can."

"Can't wait," Prue muttered.

Phoebe slumped on the couch looking miserable. "Your heart-to-heart with Kenji didn't go well?" Prue guessed.

"We didn't have one," Phoebe reported. "The minute I hit the pavement, he bolted. I called his name, but he didn't stop. I couldn't catch up to him. I'm sure he heard me. Why didn't he stop?"

Prue had the terrible feeling that she knew why Kenji kept walking. "Phoebe," Prue prodded gently. "Why do you think he was staring in our window?"

"Well, he's not a peeping Tom," Phoebe replied defensively. "I'd know it if I was dating a pervert."

"How about a member of the coven?"

Phoebe shut her eyes, and Prue watched the color drain from her sister's face. "I can't believe Kenji would do anything to harm me."

"In the dojo—do you know for certain that whoever attacked you wasn't Kenji?" Prue asked.

"I'm positive!" Phoebe snapped. "Sensei broke that guy's arm. I just saw Kenji, and his arms were fine."

"Then why was he staring in our living room window? And why would he avoid you?"

"I don't know." Phoebe looked miserable

again. "Because I blew it somehow?" She punched a cushion. "I was sure this time it was for real, Prue. I was even taking it *slow* so I wouldn't ruin things."

Prue bit back a smile. For Phoebe to actually slow things down, Kenji must have seemed pretty special to her. She placed a hand on her sister's shoulder. "Don't worry. You'll get over it, Phoeb."

Phoebe gave her a halfhearted smile. "You win some, you lose most of 'em."

Prue paced the living room again. "We have to do something. We have to protect ourselves against the Coven of the New Sun."

Phoebe nodded. "Let's go up to the attic and try the protection spell again. Where's Piper?"

"Helping Celeste pack so she can move in here," Prue answered.

"What?" Phoebe shrieked.

"I talked with her about it," Prue explained. "I don't think we have any other choice." Prue glanced at the green velvet pillow on the couch and summoned a small jolt of her power—just enough to send the pillow to the far end of the couch.

Instead, the pillow flew toward her, and hit her smack in the stomach.

Phoebe winced. "That was not the desired result, was it?"

"No." Prue fought back a feeling of dread. "I think we'd better scratch that protection spell," she said. "It would probably only set off an attack."

"So what now?" Phoebe asked. "Who do you call when your spells backfire?"

"How about another white witch?" Prue suggested.

"Do you know another white witch?" Phoebe seemed shocked.

Prue nodded. "Adrienne, from the Wicca store. She's got these innate powers—just like we do—and—"

"Prue—" Phoebe began.

"Look, I know that telling anyone else about us is a risk, but we're in serious danger here. Besides, Adrienne's totally opposed to any kind of black magic. She's trying her best to fight it—just like we are. And I trust her."

Phoebe shrugged. "Call her."

Prue snagged the phone from its cradle and dialed the numbers. She felt better as soon as she heard Adrienne's greeting.

"Blessed be."

"Adrienne, it's Prue," she began. "My sisters and I are in trouble. We are in serious need of some of your witching expertise and advice."

"What's the problem?" Adrienne asked.

"I can't explain over the phone," Prue said. "I'd have to show you. Can Phoebe and I come over—like, now?"

Adrienne hesitated a moment. "Yes, come over. I know I can help you. But you'll have to hurry."

"We're on our way," Prue told her.

Prue and Phoebe rushed down the alleyway that led to Full Moon. It hadn't taken them that long to get to Twenty-fourth Street, but they'd wasted a precious five minutes finding a parking space.

"Down here," Prue told Phoebe.

They descended the three steps that led to the shop and opened the door.

"Um—Prue? It's kind of dark in here," Phoebe noted in a wary voice.

Prue scanned the shop. Phoebe was right. It was unusually dark, and Adrienne was nowhere in sight. "Maybe there was a problem with the lighting," Prue suggested. But her uneasy feeling wouldn't go away. Everything was in its place, and yet the shop felt . . . wrong. The air itself felt different—dense and menacing.

"Adrienne?" Prue called uncertainly. "Are you here?"

Adrienne didn't answer, but Prue heard a muffled sound coming from behind a door at the back of the shop. Prue's heart gave a loud thump. She and Phoebe exchanged nervous glances.

"What does that door lead to?" Phoebe asked in a low voice.

"I don't know," Prue answered softly.

"I think we'd better check it out," Phoebe said.

The two sisters crept to the back of the shop. Phoebe grabbed an athame from one of the shelves.

"What are you doing with that?" Prue whispered.

"It can't hurt to be prepared," Phoebe whispered back.

Prue realized her sister had a point. She

grabbed one as well, though it didn't give her much comfort. Daggers were not her style.

More sounds came from the room behind the door. Were those sounds of a struggle? Prue felt a cold thread of fear tighten around her heart. If Adrienne was in trouble, how were they going to help her—especially with their powers gone?

Phoebe threw open the door.

Prue gasped at the sight inside. Adrienne lay struggling on her back, her arms spread out and staked down, her ankles tied together. Cold terror swept through Prue as she realized Adrienne was bound not by ropes, but by strands of glowing green light.

"Adrienne!" Prue cried.

"Ah, the Charmed Ones," a voice growled.

Two cloaked figures stepped out from the shadows. Their hoods concealed their faces, but Prue recognized the inverted pentagrams around their necks and athames tied at their waists. She had seen them in *The Book of Shadows*. There was no doubt—she and Phoebe were face-to-face with two members of the Coven of the New Sun.

The figure nearest Prue spoke. "We were hoping you'd show up. But someone is missing. Where is the third sister?"

"Don't tell them anything!" Adrienne cried.

"You don't learn, do you?" The shorter warlock made a raking gesture in the air above Adrienne's chest. Adrienne screamed and lines of bright red blood welled through the pale yellow dress she wore, as if he'd sliced her skin with talons.

Prue snapped out of her shock. Normally, she'd just blast these warlocks into the bay. But today that wasn't an option. Not with her compromised power. Running wasn't the answer either. She couldn't leave Adrienne. She and Phoebe were going to have to improvise—fast.

Prue stepped forward, hoping to bluff her way through. "You were hoping we'd show up?" she declared boldly. "We're so flattered. And we'd really love to visit with you, but first"—she gestured toward Adrienne—"let her go."

"I'm afraid that's not possible," the taller of the two warlocks answered. "This one has betrayed us. She has earned her death."

"Betrayed?" Prue echoed. What did the warlock mean?

He drew a loop in the air, and a rope of glowing green light materialized and looped itself around Adrienne's neck. Prue saw her friend's face contort with terror.

The warlock closed his fists as if on an invisible rope and made a sharp jerking motion. Beneath him, the rope of green light circling Adrienne's throat tightened.

Adrienne made a horrified choking sound, her face turning a ghastly shade of purple.

"Stop it!" Phoebe screamed.

Prue reached out, grabbing a box of polished crystal balls from the shelf beside her. She hurled them at the warlocks. Phoebe took the cue, sending two bronze braziers flying.

Prue ducked and bent over Adrienne. She tried

to slice through the ropes of green light with the athame she'd taken from the shop. But the ceremonial knife merely passed through the light, its silver blade flashing green.

Prue frantically thought of an unbinding spell. She opened her mouth to speak, then stopped herself, remembering what had happened the last time she'd attempted to use her powers. She was going to have to try something else—and pray that it would work.

"Ropes that bind, bind tighter still, confound me not, obey my will," she whispered over Adrienne.

Just as she had hoped, the ropes of green light dissolved. Her spell had backfired—exactly the way she'd wanted it to. "Can you run if we keep them busy?" she asked Adrienne. She risked a quick glance upward. Phoebe was holding off the two warlocks with a crowbar.

Taking deep, ragged breaths, Adrienne nodded. Prue helped her to her feet. "Run!" Prue urged.

Adrienne stumbled toward the door, and Prue turned to face her attackers. The taller warlock was down; Phoebe must have connected. But Phoebe and the shorter warlock were locked in a struggle for the crowbar—and Phoebe was losing.

One more spell in reverse, Prue thought. "Unbind these two who—"

The taller warlock got to his feet and charged Phoebe, his dagger drawn.

"No!" Prue shouted, sending a magical blast at him to fling him away from her sister. In a heartbeat, she realized her horrible mistake. Her telekinesis had reversed! She'd sent the warlock flying at Phoebe with such force it knocked them both to the floor, the tall warlock on top of her.

A strong arm wrapped around Prue's throat. "You're not only beautiful, you're helpful," the shorter warlock crooned. He held the tip of the dagger to her throat. Prue turned her head away from his stinking breath, fighting back tears. Not only had she not helped her sister, she'd gotten them both captured.

CHAPTER
15

Piper, where were you?" Celeste asked anxiously, when Piper finally made it up to her room. "I was beginning to think you'd changed your mind."

Piper shook her head. "No way. I spent the last half hour waiting to clear things with Mr. Morgan, but he wasn't around. I left him a note."

A smile lit Celeste's face. "Does that mean I can go home with you now?"

"We'll probably have to come back here, talk to Mr. Morgan, and—"

"Evaluate," Celeste filled in. "Morgan is big on evaluating."

"Yes, but you can absolutely come home with me." Piper smiled at her.

The wariness came back into Celeste's eyes. "Your sisters—they're okay with this?"

"Prue knows and understands. I haven't had a chance to tell Phoebe yet, but she's a sweetie. She'll be fine with it."

"Thank you, Piper," Celeste said.

"You're welcome. So are you packed and ready to go?"

"No." Celeste stared at the floor.

"Why not?"

"I thought that if I packed my bag . . . then it might not really happen," she mumbled.

"You were afraid I'd disappoint you," Piper translated, her heart going out to the girl. She was going to have to be very careful, she realized. Beneath Celeste's street smarts was an incredibly vulnerable kid.

Piper touched Celeste's arm, unsure of whether that was too much or not enough physical affection. "Hey, it's okay," she told her. "You haven't known me very long. You've got every right to be cautious. But I'm here now, and you're going to come stay at my house. So let's get packed. Deal?"

"Deal!" Celeste opened her closet and pulled out the worn suitcase and her jacket.

"Can I help?" asked Piper, opening a dresser drawer. She didn't want to be away from the house too long. She pulled out a T-shirt—and stopped in astonishment. "Celeste." She tried to steady her voice. "Do you know what these are?"

"What?"

Piper realized she didn't even want to touch the small pile of red ribbons. Each ribbon was knotted in the middle—identical to the ones she and her sisters had received.

Celeste peered into the drawer. "Where did those come from?"

"You don't know?"

Celeste shook her head. "Never seen 'em before. They must be Daria's."

Piper sank down onto the bottom bunk. Her earlier suspicions were dead on. Daria was definitely mixed up in the Coven of the New Sun. These ribbons proved it.

Piper's mind flashed back to the day she caught Daria on the stairs to the attic. Maybe the girl had gone in there after all. Maybe she'd even tampered with *The Book of Shadows*, reversing their powers.

Piper put her head in her hands. How could she have invited a warlock into their home? If anything happened to Phoebe or Prue now, it would be her fault.

"Piper, are you okay?" Celeste stood beside her, looking worried.

"I'm fine." Piper got to her feet. "But I need to get home and talk to my sisters."

"About me?"

"No, about Daria. Are you almost packed?"

Celeste nodded. "I'm ready if you are. Let's get out of here."

Traffic was barely moving as Piper drove back to Halliwell Manor. She found herself cursing every red light and stop sign. Is the Department of Transportation doing construction on every single street in the city today? she wondered.

"Piper?" Celeste's voice pulled her out of her antitraffic funk. "Why do you have to talk to your sisters about Daria? Do you want her to move in, too?"

The question nearly made Piper drive up onto a curb. "*No*," she said emphatically. She took a breath. "Celeste, you know that something strange has been going on with Daria. Well, those red ribbons I found in your drawer—they're used in black magic."

"How do you know?" Celeste asked.

"I had a roommate in college who was into the dark arts," Piper lied smoothly. "It's one reason that I've been so worried about Daria. I saw what getting involved in that stuff did to a good friend."

"What happened to her? Did she turn into a demon?" Celeste asked in a goofy voice, joking around.

Piper decided to sidestep that one. It was crazy to go on spinning a lie when there were some truths that the girl had a right to know. "Phoebe and Prue and I all found ribbons like that yesterday. Mine was in my purse. Someone had to have put it there."

"Well . . . that's weird and all," Celeste admitted. "But how come it's got you so wigged out?"

Piper had to choose her words carefully now. "From what I know about black magic," she said, "those ribbons are kind of a calling card. Sort of announcing that someone is after you."

"This is ridiculous. Why would Daria be after you and your sisters?"

"I'm not sure. And, actually, I'm not sure that Daria is the only one who's after us." She paused. "Celeste, I want you to realize—you may not be any safer at my house than you were at the center."

Celeste gazed out the window, silent.

"Celeste, did you hear me?"

Piper stopped for yet another red light, and the girl turned to face her. "I heard you. And I won't lie, Daria scares the hell out of me. But I'd still rather be with you at your house than rooming with her at the center."

"Okay," Piper said. It didn't make things any better, but at least Celeste knew that she still had to be on guard—that Halliwell Manor might not be the safe haven that Piper so desperately wanted it to be.

Piper finally pulled up in front of the house. She grabbed Celeste's suitcase, climbed the stairs, and unlocked the door. "Anyone home?" she called. She stepped into the foyer. Afternoon sunlight streamed across the polished wood floor. "Prue? Phoebe?"

Celeste followed her in. "I forgot how big this place was," she said, sounding awed.

"Uh-huh," Piper murmured. She wasn't sure why, but the fact that Prue and Phoebe had left the house gave her a bad feeling. The place was too quiet. Don't be crazy, she scolded herself. You've come home to an empty house zillions of times.

"So where do I put my things?" Celeste asked.

"Second floor. Come on, I'll show you." Piper led the way upstairs.

I'll put a call into Buckland's to see if Prue is there, she thought, trying to calm herself with a rational plan. Then maybe I can try the dojo and ask if anyone's seen Phoebe.

Piper opened the door to the guest room. The twin bed was still covered with Gram's chenille bedspread. A photograph of their mother as a little girl hung over the chest of drawers. A vase of faded paper flowers stood atop the oak bookcase, and an old overstuffed easy chair sat in the corner by the window.

"This is nice," Celeste said.

"It's not the Hilton, but it's comfy," Piper agreed. "You can put your stuff in the dresser or in the closet," Piper said. "Feel free to borrow books, raid the fridge, watch TV, whatever. Make yourself at home."

Celeste put her suitcase on the bed. "Thanks."

Piper suddenly felt like she was being a lousy host. "Are you hungry? Want me to fix you a sandwich or—"

"I'm fine," Celeste was smiling now. "Really, Piper, I am."

"Okay, then I'm going downstairs to make some phone calls," Piper told her. "Yell if you need anything."

"I will," Celeste promised.

Piper started down the stairs. She'd feel a lot better once she talked to her sisters. She stopped on the landing as she heard an unfamiliar noise. Was that Celeste moving around her room?

No, the sound wasn't coming from the second floor. It was coming from upstairs. From the attic.

Her heart in her throat, Piper climbed the stairs. She tried to move soundlessly. It couldn't be Celeste, she told herself. No, she heard Celeste humming in her room as she passed the second floor.

Piper stopped. Maybe, if someone *was* in the attic, it wasn't such a smart idea to go up there without any means of defense. Especially now when her powers were totally unreliable.

Reversing direction, Piper went back down to the ground floor, grabbed the iron poker from the fireplace, and started up the stairs again. She heard the noises again. Something was definitely in the attic. Please let it be a raccoon, she prayed.

She stopped for a moment, her mind racing feverishly. Maybe what she ought to do was just get Celeste out of the house and run as fast and far as they could.

Then she knew she couldn't. *The Book of Shadows* was in the attic. She couldn't risk letting that fall into the wrong hands.

Piper climbed to the third floor, her hands wrapped tightly around the metal poker. The attic door was closed. She couldn't tell if that was good or bad.

Bracing herself, she twisted the knob and pushed open the door. Her heart nearly stopped when she saw the three figures in long black hooded robes, standing around the lectern that held the closed *Book of Shadows*.

Piper inched into the attic, holding the poker like a baseball bat. She wanted to scream a warning to Celeste, but that would be like sending a neon announcement to the warlocks: Guess what? There's someone else you can torture on the second floor.

One of the warlocks whirled around. Piper let out a gasp.

"Fascinating book you have here." The warlock tilted his head, indicating *The Book of Shadows*. "Perhaps you'd like to show it to us."

Piper felt a smug smile cross her lips as she understood what had happened. The warlocks had tried to open *The Book of Shadows*, but the book's own power was protecting it; it wouldn't open.

"Get out of here," Piper ordered, trying not to reveal her fear.

"Are you so rude to all your guests?" one of the other warlocks inquired.

The three of them closed in on Piper. She swiped at them with the poker. They advanced, undeterred. "Don't worry. We'll take the book with us," one warlock told the others.

"I don't think so." Piper swung the poker again.

The three hooded figures rushed at her. "No!" she screamed. Without thinking, she raised her hands to freeze time—and found herself completely immobilized. The three warlocks surrounded her. Laid their hands on her.

Piper heard them laugh and felt her stiff body being lifted onto their shoulders. Then everything went black.

CHAPTER
16

Piper struggled to open her eyes. She was standing in a space so dark that she couldn't see. Her mind felt groggy, her body heavy and numb. She flexed her fingers. They worked. The time-freeze was definitely over. She tried to lift her arm, but couldn't. Her arms were bound behind her back.

Piper tried not to panic. Where was she? How much time had passed since the three warlocks had taken her from the house? And what had happened to Celeste? Had they gotten her, too? Piper prayed the girl had somehow escaped. Oh, Celeste, I'm so sorry I ever got you mixed up in this, she thought.

As for Prue and Phoebe . . . Piper desperately hoped they were somewhere nearby, plotting to free her.

Piper strained to see into the surrounding

darkness. She couldn't tell if she was in a building or a cave. Wherever she was, the air was bitingly cold and damp. Piper shivered. An overwhelming wave of nausea and weakness went through her.

Instantly Piper knew exactly where she was—in the abandoned house on Colwood Street. Terror made it hard for her to breathe. She had never wanted to come back to this place. Something inside told her she'd never be lucky enough to escape it twice.

Piper heard a loud crackling sound. Two torches blazed up beside her. She squinted against the sudden blinding light.

The torches illuminated two ends of an altar draped in black cloth. A huge bronze urn sat in the center of the altar, giving off a sickeningly sweet smoke.

Piper craned her neck, peering to her right. An army of warlocks, all draped in identical black hooded robes, surrounded her. They wore athames at their waists and inverted pentagrams on their chests. A large white crystal hung in the center of the room. Fear shook her. She was, she had no doubt, in the heart of the Coven of the New Sun.

A tall warlock moved behind the altar. He clapped his hands together and candles set in sconces on the walls came to life, flickering across the cavernous room.

She glanced to her left and cried out in dismay. Her sisters were standing next to her, their hands magically bound behind them by strands of glowing red light.

"Piper!" Prue gasped.

"No! I can't believe they've gotten us all," Phoebe moaned.

Piper's weakness and terror were replaced by anger. She turned toward the leader of the coven. "Who are you?" she demanded. "Why are you doing this to us?"

"You may address me as Master," the coven leader instructed.

"Master of what?" Piper spat. "Hokey Halloween costumes?"

One of the hooded warlocks stepped forward and slapped Piper's face. The sting of it only increased her anger.

"Perhaps that will teach you to be more grateful. After all, I have reunited you with your precious sisters," the Master growled.

"Where's Celeste?" Piper demanded.

"All in good time. All your questions shall all be answered in good time." The Master's voice was familiar, Piper realized, but she couldn't quite place it. Who was he?

"Let us begin," the Master instructed his followers. Several warlocks moved about the room, lighting incense. A low, droning chant filled the room. A woman was carried into the room. Who was she? Piper noticed her long blond braid. It was Adrienne, the woman from the Wicca shop!

"Set her down," the tall warlock ordered.

Adrienne was again laid out on the floor. This

time ropes of red light bound her. She wasn't struggling; in fact, she barely seemed conscious.

The warlocks continued their low, rhythmic chant. It increased in volume.

"What are they doing?" Phoebe whispered to Prue.

"I don't know," Prue replied.

The chant rose in pitch. Piper could feel the energy in the room grow darker, stronger. Adrienne began to writhe and whimper. Her cries became screams as her body convulsed. A sickening stench of burned flesh and hair filled the room as her skin began to bubble. It melted and peeled back from her bones.

Piper turned away from the horror. She glanced over at Phoebe, whose eyes were shut tight. Prue's expression was hard, but Piper could see the tears streaming down her face.

Piper's heart went out to her sister. Prue had considered Adrienne a friend.

Piper forced herself to take one last look at Adrienne. Her hair had singed off. Her flesh was bubbling, sliding from her bones. There was no trace of the beautiful woman she had been before.

The Master turned to face them. "Consider this an education, Charmed Ones. You've witnessed the price that must be paid by those who oppose the Coven of the New Sun."

Phoebe glared up at him. "Is that what you're going to do to us?"

The warlock merely chuckled.

"Answer me!" she shouted.

"You're hardly in a position to make demands. We will deal with you soon enough," the Master mocked them.

Piper kept her eyes on her sisters. Prue's ice-blue eyes were hard with anger, and Phoebe looked like she'd gladly tear a warlock to shreds. Her sisters were as determined to fight the coven as she was. But how? If there was any chance of them getting out of this alive, they were going to have to use the Power of Three, a power that, inverted by the coven's magic, might only make everything worse.

"You Halliwells are so spirited." The Master stepped down from his place behind the altar. "It's almost a shame that you have to be destroyed. But you see, we must kill you because you have pitted yourselves against us. You have committed your power to doing good." He stood next to another warlock—the one nearest to Piper. "The ironic part is that we have used your inclination for good to trap you—all of you."

In a flash he pulled down the hood of the warlock beside him, so that her face was revealed.

Piper gasped, stricken. She fought to breathe, unable to believe her eyes. She took in the delicate features—the short, reddish hair. The young warlock before her—was Celeste!

Piper stared, trying to wrap her brain around the fact that this girl whom she cared about—whom she had tried to protect—had been bent on destroying her from the start.

Piper turned to her sisters. "I'm so sorry," she told them.

"Piper, I—" Celeste began.

"I just want to know one thing," Piper snapped, interrupting her. "Was any of what you told me true? Or was absolutely everything a lie?" She hated herself for sounding so hurt, but she needed to understand. If she and her sisters were going to die tonight, she wanted to know exactly what it was they were dying for.

Celeste frowned. "Most of it was true. I really am an orphan—and I really have lived in about a million foster homes. And I did get snagged by the police."

"What about Daria? Where is she? Is she the one who led you into this?"

A wry smile played across Celeste's face. "You still don't get it, do you?" she said. "Daria's only problem was that I was her roommate. The minute I saw her, I knew I could use her. With that huge chip on her shoulder, I knew she'd be difficult. When she ran out of your house, it was the absolute perfect opportunity to distract you. I fed you all those stories about her and planted witchy props around our room, all so you'd have no idea of what I was doing." She paused, the smile fading from her face. "I guess it worked."

"Why?" Piper demanded. "Why would you do this to us?"

"Why?" Celeste gestured toward the figures that surrounded them. "Because I had no one, and the coven took me in."

"Celeste is part of our family," the Master said. He removed his hood, and Piper drew in a deep breath, recognizing the salt-and-pepper hair, the green eyes. No wonder he sounded so familiar.

"M-Mr. Morgan?" she stuttered.

"Working as the director of the Sunrise Center is so very convenient," he explained smoothly. "Every week new children come to us, all of them homeless, desperate to belong, aching for family. The coven gives them just that, for a small price, of course—allegiance to our cause for life."

Piper recoiled. She could barely bring herself to look at this—this monster who took advantage of vulnerable kids.

"Celeste is one of my most promising acolytes," the Master went on. "A gifted actress who is truly adept at magic. So you needn't berate yourself, Piper. You were outclassed from the start. And if it's any comfort, you're in excellent company. After all, your sister Prue got herself and Phoebe captured trying to save Adrienne. Apparently, it never occurred to them that she was one of us as well."

Piper saw the fury in Prue's eyes.

"Yes," the Master went on. "Adrienne was one of my spiders, sent to lure you into my web. Unfortunately, she began to weaken and turned traitor at the end. So we had no choice. We had to destroy her.

"As we shall now destroy you."

CHAPTER 17

If i could just get out of these ropes—or whatever they are—Phoebe thought, I'd rip that guy apart! She strained against the magical binding at her wrists.

Mr. Morgan was evil, pure evil. Phoebe knew he had to be stopped. She struggled harder. It was no use. She was completely powerless.

"Let's see . . . which of you three would like to die first?" Mr. Morgan asked in a genial tone. He waited a moment. "No volunteers? Then I shall have to choose."

Phoebe hated him more with every second. She hated what he'd done to her sisters, to the kids at the Sunrise Center, and even to Adrienne. Most of all, she hated his cruelty. There has to be a way to fight him, she thought. We can't give in.

The Master waved a finger back and forth in front of the sisters' faces. "Eeney, meeney, miney . . ." It stopped in front of Phoebe. "Mo!" he announced. "It seems that you've won."

Phoebe felt her heart constrict with fear. The Master clapped his hands. "Bring her to the New Sun," he ordered.

Two tall, powerful warlocks grabbed each of Phoebe's arms. She twisted her body, trying to wriggle out of their grasp. They dragged her toward the center of the room, where they set her beneath a large, suspended white crystal, facing the Master.

"No!" Prue cried.

The Master began to chant again. Phoebe watched him pour vials of colored powder into the bronze urn that sat on the altar before him. The smell from the urn became even more foul as he added roots and oils and a handful of herbs.

Pale green smoke swirled up from the urn. The Master raised his hands, his fingers outstretched. Phoebe didn't know exactly what he was doing, but she had a strong feeling that it was so not good.

Bright green lightning began to dance along the Master's fingertips. It flickered upward, then arced out across the room to the crystal. The lightning sizzled around the clear white stone. Seconds later the stone began to glow.

"When you die, the New Sun shall absorb your energy and then feed it back to the coven. A sort of recycling, if you will." Mr. Morgan smirked at Phoebe.

The crystal's glow intensified. Phoebe shut her eyes as waves of power shimmered from it, and it began to give off a dazzling, bright white heat. Sweat poured down Phoebe's back and chest. She felt her skin reddening, stinging with heat.

"Phoebe!" Piper screamed.

The Master began another of his droning chants, and this time the coven joined in. The crystal dropped lower, and glowed whiter, hotter. Phoebe felt her skin burn and blister. She smelled an awful smell as her hair and eyelashes singed.

Then Phoebe heard Piper's voice over the chants. "Celeste!" Piper pleaded. "You can't let them do this. They don't care about you like I do. They're only using you for your power. Don't let them do this to my sister!"

The chanting continued, and the light of the New Sun grew stronger.

"Please!" Piper was practically sobbing.

Phoebe moaned in pain as her blisters began to split open.

"Wait," Phoebe heard Celeste mumble.

The chanting droned on.

"Wait!" Celeste ordered, her voice stronger this time. The voices of the coven faltered.

"What are you stopping for? Continue!" the Master commanded.

"I said *wait!*" Celeste thundered. The sound of the chant died altogether.

Phoebe's pain abated. She glanced up at Celeste. The girl held her hands outward. A glow emanated from her palms. All eyes were riveted on her. Phoebe realized Celeste was working some kind of powerful magic. It was weakening the hold that the crystal had over her. She moved her wrists. Her hands were free!

No one noticed—the entire room was focused on Celeste.

"Foolish girl! You would disobey me now?" the Master demanded, furious.

"I thought you'd be used to rebellious teens by now, Mr. Morgan," Celeste mocked him.

It was the perfect distraction. Phoebe reached up to the nearest warlock and gently removed the athame that was belted to his waist. She crawled through the crowded room and stopped directly behind her sisters.

She began to murmur an unbinding spell. Wait, she thought, our powers are still reversed. Instead, she recited:

> Magic strands with power true,
> Never fail to bind these two.

The strands of light entwining her sisters' wrists dissolved. Yes! It worked!

"They're getting away!" Phoebe heard a voice shout. She gasped as someone grabbed her from behind. His arms locked around her.

Self-defense combination number one, Phoebe ordered herself. She moved her arms in a scissors strike, pushing her attacker's arms apart. Then she came down hard on his instep with her heel, pivoted, and swept his ankle, taking him down.

I did it! she thought in shock. Awesome!

Phoebe spun around. A warlock built like Frankenstein's monster charged straight for her, his knife raised. "Aaaah!" she yelped. If there was a self-defense combination for this, she hadn't learned it yet.

As the warlock rushed at her, she tucked herself into a ball, ducked to the side, and stuck out her foot.

The warlock tripped. Phoebe watched wide-eyed as his momentum carried him over her. His body slammed into the white crystal.

The huge stone ripped from its chain in the ceiling. It crashed into one of the walls, then skittered across the floor.

"Nooo!" the Master cried. "Get it! Get the crystal!" Every warlock in the room ran for the stone, but no one seemed able to overcome its power long enough to hold it.

Now what? Phoebe wondered. She assumed a fighting stance and cast a quick glance around the chaotic room, searching for her sisters.

They were only a few feet away. Celeste was standing in front of them, her palm outstretched. She held three knotted red ribbons. Phoebe ran to join them.

"Magic that binds will now unbind," Celeste chanted. "Restore their powers in full and in kind."

Phoebe felt a surge of power rush into her. A familiar sense of light and strength traveled from her feet up through her body to the top of her head. It filled her and healed her burns. More than that, it gave her a sense of connection to her sisters that she knew was the source of her strength.

Piper turned toward her. "Phoebe, you're okay!"

"We all are," Prue said. "Our powers are back!"

"Thanks to Celeste," Piper said.

Celeste stared at Piper. Tears brimmed in her eyes. "I thought they were my family, but they never cared about me the way you did." She sobbed. "You risked your life for me. I'm so sorry I did this to you."

Piper put her arms around the weeping girl.

"We believe you," Prue said hurriedly, "but let's discuss this later, okay?"

Phoebe glanced around the room. The confusion had calmed, and angry warlocks now surrounded the four girls.

"Sure," Phoebe commented. "If there is a later."

Piper gulped as the circle of furious warlocks tightened. "We are so outnumbered," she mumbled.

"It looks like a fair fight to me," Prue said. "Let's kick some warlock butt." She fixed her gaze on the twelve or so warlocks who were directly in front of them.

Whoosh! All twelve blasted into the far wall of

the room, taking down others in their path. "Yes! That felt good!"

Piper saw a warlock behind Phoebe, his athame upraised, plunging toward her. "Stop!" She flung up her hands, freezing time.

"Thanks, Piper." Phoebe stepped forward, extracted the blade from her attacker's hand, and kicked him solidly in the groin. As the time-freeze faded, the warlock doubled over in agony.

"That was very satisfying," Phoebe commented.

Prue whirled around and sent another group of warlocks flying across the room and crashing through the boards that covered the windows.

"Enough!" the Master's voice thundered through the room.

"I don't think so," Piper told him. "We've barely started."

Prue blasted him against the wall behind the altar.

"Uh, Prue," Phoebe murmured. "I think that might have been a mistake."

The Master had peeled himself off the wall. A circle of crimson light surrounded him, crackling with power. Piper blinked, wondering if her eyes were playing tricks on her. Within the circle of red light, the Master's form was elongating like a shadow. He was growing larger—more powerful. The Master had turned into a huge, skeletal monster. He advanced on the Charmed Ones.

Piper felt her courage waning. She'd fought plenty of shapeshifters, but this was different. She'd never seen anything take on this sort of form. It was something straight out of her worst nightmare. Everything else in the room seemed to fade. She was dimly aware of Prue blasting more warlocks away from them, of Phoebe chanting something that made others abandon their attacks to scratch themselves furiously.

"Piper, you and I have unfinished business," the Master intoned. In two enormous strides he towered over her, the red light dancing wildly around him.

Piper trembled with fear. She reminded herself of what Mr. Morgan—now this thing—had done to Celeste and countless other young girls who'd had the misfortune to wind up at the Sunrise Center. Her anger gave her courage.

"You're right," she agreed. "I still have to destroy you and this coven."

Piper's hands flew up, freezing him. "Prue, Phoebe, I need you!" she cried.

Her sisters were at her side at once.

"I think he deserves a taste of his own medicine," Prue said. She began the words of a binding spell. Piper and Phoebe joined her. They held hands, chanting, calling on the Power of Three to reinforce the spell.

Piper felt the incredible strength that flowed through her whenever the Power of Three was invoked. "Bind him hard, bind him fast," she chanted with her sisters. "Throughout time shall this spell last."

A thick cord of pure white light twisted itself around the Master's body and the circle of red light that surrounded him, as though wrapping a mummy.

The time-freeze ended. The white strands of light began to flicker and fade. The spell, Piper realized. It wasn't working!

"Silly girls!" the Master boomed. "Your magic is nothing compared to mine. You cannot stop me."

"But this can!" Celeste shouted.

She stood in front of the altar, holding the white crystal in her hands.

The Master whirled to face her. "Put that down!" he screamed.

"Gladly," Celeste said, and dropped it into the giant smoking bronze urn.

"Noooo!" The Master lurched toward her, but Celeste was unfazed. "The fire will purify the crystal," she reminded him. "It will transform its power from evil to good."

"You'll destroy us all!" the Master roared, racing toward the urn. "Including yourself!"

"Maybe," Celeste said, her mouth a grim line. "But I'm willing to take that chance."

The Master shoved her away from the altar and plunged his hands into the bubbling urn. He cried out in agony as he lifted out the crystal.

It glowed in his hands brighter than ever. The

Master strained to hold on to it. Sweat beaded his brow. His hands began to blister.

"Say bye-bye," Celeste told him. She gave him a little wave.

"Aaahhhhh!" the Master screeched. Piper was knocked to the ground as the crystal exploded into a million pieces.

CHAPTER
18

The sound of the explosion grew louder, so loud that Piper thought her eardrums might shatter. She curled up in a ball, her eyes shut, her hands over her ears, praying that the terrible pressure would pass.

Then, with the rumble of a wave being drawn back out to sea, it was gone. Piper waited a moment before sitting up and looking around. The wave of magic had taken all of the warlocks with it. The only ones who were left in the house on Colwood Street were the Charmed Ones—and Celeste.

Piper ran toward her. "Thank goodness, you're all right!" she cried, throwing her arms around her.

Celeste hugged her back.

"Because I'd been a warlock for so long, I

174

wasn't sure the crystal's good energy would let me live," Celeste admitted. "I kept waiting for it to destroy me. But I think—I think that helping you guys saved me."

"That was some impressive mojo, girl," Phoebe said.

Celeste shuddered. "I don't ever want to work magic again as long as I live."

Prue frowned. "Are you sure? You've obviously got a gift. And power like yours used for good—"

"Please," Celeste said. "Using magic will only remind me of being in the coven, of being taken in by evil. I need to get as far away from that as I can. I want a nice, normal life."

"Well, the three of us may not qualify as normal," Piper quipped, "but we'll always be there for you."

"Thanks." Celeste smiled. Her eyes moved to the doorway. Her face paled.

"What is it?" Piper asked.

Celeste pointed. Another figure in a black robe stepped into the room. "It's not over!"

The figure pulled back his hood. Phoebe gasped. "Kenji!"

Was this the man Phoebe had told her about? Piper wondered. If so, what was he doing here?

"He's one of them!" Celeste shouted. "He's trying to trap you! We have to destroy him!"

Prue wasted no time. She sent a blast of energy at Kenji that pinned him to the wall. Kenji struggled against the power, trying furiously to wrench himself free.

Prue walked up to him, her power still holding him to the wall. She glanced at Phoebe. "Do you want me to kill him for you?" she asked.

"No!" Kenji screamed.

"Why not?" Phoebe demanded. Her eyes filled with tears. Her voice gave away the hurt she felt. "You used me. You made me believe you cared about me! And all the time you were a warlock plotting to destroy us!"

"I'm not a warlock!" Kenji answered.

"Funny, but you sure look like one," Phoebe said. "Black robe, dagger at the waist, upside-down necklace . . ."

"I'm a reporter," he insisted. "A magazine journalist on assignment to infiltrate the coven and expose it."

"What?" For a moment Phoebe looked ready to accept Kenji's explanation. Then she crossed her arms over her chest. "Why on earth should we believe that?"

"Because it's true," Kenji told her. "It's why I was spying through your window the other day." He looked at Prue. "If you'll release me, I can show you my press pass and ID. It's in the pocket of the shirt I'm wearing underneath this stupid robe."

"Your call," Prue said to Phoebe.

Phoebe considered for a moment. "Don't release him yet. If he decides to fight us, it would be like going up against Bruce Lee." Carefully she removed the dagger from the belt around his waist. Then, delicately but deliberately, she sliced open the black robe.

She reached into his shirt pocket and took out two laminated cards. She stared at them, stunned.

"He's telling the truth," she reported a moment later. "He's got a press pass and an ID."

"That doesn't mean anything," Celeste argued. "You told the coven that Phoebe had the power to see the future," she reminded Kenji.

"I had to cooperate to keep my cover," Kenji said quietly.

"They would have known if I'd lied. And for a long time, the Master suspected Phoebe had those powers." His eyes searched Phoebe's. "You have to believe me—I never intended to let anything bad happen to you."

He scanned the room. "What happened to the coven?"

"They're gone. For good," Prue said.

Kenji's eyes widened. "Did you three . . . ?"

"We four, actually," Piper said, putting an arm around Celeste.

"Wow," Kenji said softly. "That must have been major magic."

"Yeah. So, great—you have your story," Phoebe said bitterly.

Kenji smiled broadly. "And it's the story of a lifetime!" Phoebe turned her back on him. "But I never meant you any harm! I swear it."

"I really liked you, Kenji," Phoebe said in a small voice. "I didn't think you were using me—for whatever reason."

"I liked you, too! I liked you so much I was

going to ask my editor to transfer me to San Francisco as soon as I got this story in."

Slowly Phoebe turned around. "You were going to move to San Francisco? For me?"

Kenji nodded. "I realized that I didn't want to leave you, Phoebe. You're just too special." He smiled. "And I don't just mean because of your powers."

Prue cleared her throat loudly. "I hate to interrupt this," she said, "but it's time for a little sister conference here."

Phoebe gave Kenji a lingering look, then went to join her sisters on the opposite side of the room.

"He's willing to move here—for me!" Phoebe told her sisters.

Piper gave her a sympathetic look. "We heard. And I'm really glad for you, Phoeb," she said. "But there's just one little problem. We can't let him publish his story."

"It would ruin us completely," Prue agreed.

"Right," Phoebe said, biting her lip.

"I have an idea. Let's cast a 'forget' spell on him," Prue suggested. "Just so that he'll forget we're witches. That way, he can still write the exposé about the coven—without exposing us in the process."

"You mean I get to keep the guy, and he gets to keep his story?" Phoebe smiled. "Sound like a plan. Let's do it." The sisters joined hands and began to chant.

*   *   *

The next night Phoebe stood outside the door to Kenji's Berkeley apartment. She hesitated before knocking and glanced down at herself, wishing she had a mirror. She was wearing a short black dress and Prue's classy silver earrings. Did she look all right? She hoped so.

She checked the contents of the two shopping bags that she was carrying. The first contained Piper's special "catered" meal: slices of roast beef au jus, to-die-for garlic mashed potatoes, and a Caesar salad. The second bag held candles, candlesticks, flowers, and a bottle of wine. All the ingredients for a perfect, romantic dinner. She planned on making this a night that the two of them would remember. The official start of their warlock-free relationship.

Kenji, of course, didn't know he was in for a romantic dinner. This was one of Phoebe's spontaneous surprises. She knocked on the door, eager with anticipation.

She heard the locks turn from the inside. "Hey," Kenji said in a soft voice.

"Hey, yourself," she answered. She looked him over. His long, gleaming black hair hung loose, and the jeans and a black T-shirt that he was wearing showed off his well-defined arms and chest. He looked incredibly hot. "How are you doing?" she asked.

"Good," he answered. He smiled at her, his eyes filled with warmth. "How did I luck into you showing up?"

"Well, you know. I just happened to be in the

neighborhood," she teased. She stepped into the apartment.

When Kenji closed the door, she leaned forward and pressed her lips to his. He pulled back, startled.

"What's wrong?" she asked.

"Sorry, but you took me by surprise."

"Surprise?" Phoebe laughed. "Why would you think I wouldn't kiss you?"

"When someone comes to check out an apartment, kissing the current tenant is usually not a requirement," he pointed out. "Not that I minded it." He smiled at her.

"Check out an apartment? Kenji, what are you talking about? You . . ." Her voice trailed off. A horrible hollow feeling formed in the pit of her stomach.

"Kenji," she asked. "What's my name?"

He gave her an amused look. "Well, I was getting around to asking, but then you leaned in and kissed me."

"You don't know me, do you?"

He shook his head. "Sorry, but no, I don't. I've only been here a little while, and I'm moving back to San Diego at the end of the week. Job-related stuff. You know how it is."

It's the spell, Phoebe realized, the forgetting spell we cast on Kenji last night. It worked, but it worked too well. Not only has Kenji forgotten I'm a witch, he's forgotten that I existed at all.

"What's wrong?" Kenji asked gently.

Phoebe blinked back tears. "Nothing," she said. "I just—I guess I have the wrong address."

Kenji smiled. "Well, can I help you find the right one? I'm usually really good with directions."

"No. That's okay." Phoebe swallowed hard. She handed him the bags with Piper's home-cooked meal, the candles, and the wine. "Here. This is for you. I've got to go."

"But—"

"Have a good life in San Diego," she told him. Then she raced out of the apartment and into the night.

She dove into the driver's seat of her car, slammed the door, and sobbed. She figured the very least she was entitled to was a good cry.

When she finally wiped away the last of her tears, she glanced into the rearview mirror. Her nose was swollen and her eyes were red. She let out a loud laugh. She looked so awful, it was comic.

Oh, well, Phoebe thought, sometimes love hurts. Especially when you're a witch.

About the Author

F. GOLDSBOROUGH has written twenty-five books for young readers. She works part time as an editor. She grew up in New Jersey and now lives in New York City.

YOU COULD WIN A DIAMOND HEART PENDANT JUST LIKE PRUE'S!

Cast Your Own Spell—Enter Now!
4 Chances to Win!

1 Grand Prize:
A diamond heart pendant just like the one
Prue wears on the show.
50 First Prizes:
A Charmed baby-doll T-shirt.

Enter now!
50 winners who enter from KISS OF DARKNESS will receive
a Charmed baby-doll T-shirt. More chances to win
in these upcoming Charmed books.

THE CRIMSON SPELL (April 2000)
WHISPERS FROM THE PAST (June 2000)
VOODOO MOON (August 2000)

Grand prize winner will be chosen from all entries received from sweepstakes in KISS OF DARKNESS,
THE CRIMSON SPELL, WHISPERS FROM THE PAST, and VOODOO MOON combined.
No purchase necessary. See details on back.

Complete entry form and send to:
Pocket Books/ "Charmed Sweepstakes"
1230 Avenue of the Americas, 13th Floor, NY, NY 10020

NAME_____ BIRTHDATE ___/___/___

ADDRESS_____

CITY_____ STATE_____ ZIP_____

PHONE_____

PARENT OR LEGAL GUARDIAN'S SIGNATURE (REQUIRED FOR ENTRANTS UNDER 18 YEARS OF AGE AT TIME OF ENTRY.)

_____

See back for official rules.   Book Code #C3

Pocket Books/"Charmed Sweepstakes"
Sponsors Official Rules:

1. No Purchase Necessary.

2. Enter by mailing this completed Official Entry Form (no copies allowed) or by mailing a 3" x 5" card with your name and address, daytime telephone number, birthdate and parent or legal guardian's signature if entrant is under 18 at date of entry to the Pocket Books/"Charmed Sweepstakes", 1230 Avenue of the Americas, 13th Floor, NY, NY 10020. Entry forms are available in the back of Charmed books KISS OF DARKNESS (2/00) Book Code #C2, THE CRIMSON SPELL (4/00) Book Code #C3, WHISPERS FROM THE PAST (6/00) Book Code #C4 and VOODOO MOON (8/00) Book Code #C5, on in-store book displays and on the Web site SimonSays.com. Sweepstakes begins 2/1/00. Please indicate the applicable book code # (i.e., C2, C3, C4, or C5) on your entry form and the envelope. Entries must be postmarked by 8/31/00 and received by 9/15/00. Not responsible for lost, late, damaged, postage-due, stolen, illegible, mutilated, incomplete, or misdirected or not delivered entries or mail or for typographical errors in the entry form or rules or for telecommunication system or computer software or hardware errors or data loss. Entries are void if they are in whole or in part illegible, incomplete or damaged. Enter as often as you wish, but each entry must be mailed separately. Grand prize winner will be selected at random from all eligible entries received. There will be 4 separate drawings for first prize winners and for each such drawing 50 winners will be chosen from all eligible entries received for each of books 2-5 in the Charmed series. Thus there will be 1 drawing for the entries received for *Kiss of Darkness* and 1 drawing for *The Crimson Spell*, etc. The drawing for grand prize and first prizes will be held on or about 9/25/00. Winners will be notified by mail. The grand prize winner will be notified by phone as well.

3. Prizes: One Grand Prize: A diamond heart pendant like Prue's (approx. retail value: $500). 200 First Prizes: A Charmed baby-doll T-shirt (approx. retail value: $8 each).

4. The sweepstakes is open to legal residents of the U.S. (excluding Puerto Rico) and Canada (excluding Quebec) ages 12-21 as of 8/31/00, except as set forth below. Proof of age is required to claim prize. Prizes will be awarded to the winner's parent or legal guardian if winner is under 18 years of age. Void wherever prohibited or restricted by law. All federal, state and local laws apply. Simon & Schuster Inc., Parachute Publishing, Spelling Television Inc. and their respective officers, directors, shareholders, employees, suppliers, parent companies, subsidiaries, affiliates, agencies, sponsors, participating retailers, and persons connected with the use, marketing or conduct of this sweepstakes are not eligible. Family members living in the same household as any of the individuals referred to in the preceding sentence are not eligible.

5. One prize per person or household. Prizes are not transferable and may not be substituted except by sponsors, in the event of prize unavailability, in which case a prize of equal or greater value will be awarded. All prizes will be awarded. The odds of winning a prize depend upon the number of eligible entries received.

6. If a winner is a Canadian resident, then he/she must correctly answer a skill-based question administered by mail.

7. All expenses on receipt and use of prize including federal, state and local taxes are the sole responsibility of the winners. Grand prize winner may be required to execute and return an Affidavit of Eligibility and Publicity Release and all other legal documents which the sweepstakes sponsor may require (including a W-9 tax form) within 15 days of attempted notification or an alternate winner will be selected.

8. Winners or winners' parents or legal guardians on winners' behalf agree to allow use of their names, photographs, likenesses, and entries for any advertising, promotion and publicity purposes without further compensation to or permission from the entrants, except where prohibited by law.

9. Winners or winners' parents or legal guardians, as applicable, agree that Simon & Schuster, Inc., Parachute Publishing and Spelling Television Inc. and their respective officers, directors, shareholders, employees, suppliers, parent companies, subsidiaries, affiliates, agencies, sponsors, participating retailers, and persons connected with the use, marketing or conduct of this sweepstakes, shall have no responsibility or liability for injuries, losses or damages of any kind in connection with the collection, acceptance or use of the prizes awarded herein, or from participation in this promotion.

10. By participating in this sweepstakes, entrants agree to be bound by these rules and the decisions of the judges and sweepstakes sponsors, which are final in all matters relating to the sweepstakes. Failure to comply with the Official Rules may result in a disqualification of your entry and prohibition of any further participation in this sweepstakes.

11. The first names of the winners will be posted at SimonSays.com (available after 9/30/00) or the names of the winners may be obtained by sending a stamped, self-addressed envelope to Prize Winners, Pocket Books "Charmed Sweepstakes," 1230 Avenue of the Americas, 13th Floor, NY, NY 10020.